THE

Praise for The Way Back Home

'Beautiful, heartbreaking, yet wonderfully funny . . .
Engaging and gripping from the get-go. Stratton writes
some of the wittiest dialogue in YA fiction today'
Susin Nielsen

'Terrific. I read it in one big gulp. Does Stratton have
an ear for dialogue or what? His splendid new novel
involves a journey from a painful past into something
like utter grace' Gary D. Schmidt

'It broke my heart and then healed it again'
Susan Juby

Praise for The Dogs

'An accomplished, gripping and thoughtful story, whose
dramatic ending delivers on every level' *Guardian*

'A darkly suspenseful thriller that blurs the lines
between reality and imagination, keeping you
guessing and keeping you awake long into the night'
The Scotsman

THE WAY BACK HOME

ALLAN STRATTON

ANDERSEN PRESS • LONDON

This edition published in 2017 by
Andersen Press Limited
20 Vauxhall Bridge Road
London SW1V 2SA
www.andersenpress.co.uk

2 4 6 8 10 9 7 5 3 1

British Library Cataloguing in Publication Data available.

ISBN 978 1 78344 521 9

Typeset in Adobe Caslon by Palimpsest Book Production Limited,
Falkirk, Stirlingshire

Printed and bound in Great Britain by Clays Limited,
Bungay, Suffolk, NR35 1ED

For

Charlie Sheppard

1

Mom's running around like a maniac, trying to make our living room look normal. Good luck with that. You can hang Walmart landscapes where the hairdo pictures go, drape nylon sheets over the dryers, and cover the sinks with trays of pretzels, but a hairdressing salon is a hair-dressing salon.

Monday to Saturday, Mom's 'gals' – 'Don't call them clients!' – gossip around the dinette set or watch TV from the dryer chairs. But today is Sunday and we're getting ready for company, which means I'm helping Dad drag the shag carpet up from his insurance office in the basement. It lives there 'cause 'Try vacuuming hair off shag all day.'

The carpet stinks worse than my principal's armpits. I'm not sure if it's from the damp concrete or Dad's sweaty feet; he takes off his shoes during panic attacks. Thank God for the fumes from Mom's rinse-sets, sprays and peppermint foot scrubs.

I lay out the carpet while Dad gets the Hide-a-Bed from the spare room so we can pretend we have a sofa. Mom's at the sink mirrors, too busy fussing with her wig to notice. She's developed 'alopecia' which is this thing where your hair falls out. Seeing as she's a hairdresser, my English teacher would call that irony. Me, I call it karma.

'Is my wig okay?'

'It's fine. People can hardly tell.'

'But they *can* tell?'

'Only if they're looking.'

Mom glares. 'You!'

'So when are we getting Granny?'

'Granny's not coming,' Dad says, wheeling in the Hide-a-Bed.

'But she's always here, Sunday dinner.'

He squeezes it between the dryers. 'Tonight's special. We don't want her upsetting Uncle Chad and Aunt Jess.'

'Granny's not welcome because of *them*?'

Mom tugs at the back of her wig. 'She'd be in that dirty plaid dress and black sweater. Lord knows how many times I've tried to wash them.'

'If you're saying Granny stinks, she doesn't. Old people don't sweat.'

'It's not only that,' Dad says. 'Who knows what she'd say?'

'The truth. Granny says what she thinks.'

'No, she *doesn't* think. That's the problem.' Dad fans a fashion magazine under his armpits.

'Enough about your granny,' Mom says. 'Get dressed.'

'I'm hardly naked.'

'Your cousin won't be wearing jeans. If you'd kept your church clothes on, there wouldn't be a problem.'

'Except I'd be dead. Who even *has* to go to church in high school?'

'Quit dawdling,' Dad says.

'Dawdling? I'm hardly three.'

'Then stop acting like it.'

Talk to my butt. I stomp to my room.

'What's gotten into her lately?' he asks Mom as if I'm deaf. 'Is it a phase?'

'Yeah. My *life* is a phase,' I toss over my shoulder and slam the door behind me. Last summer, they took my phone and grounded me for stuff I didn't even do. Now they're on about Granny all the time. And they wonder why I'm mad?

Tonight's going to be brutal. If Granny were here, we'd play footsie under the table when we were bored and try not to laugh. Without her, how will I cope? I give her a call. 'Hi, Granny.'

'Pumpkin! I was just thinking about you.'

'I was thinking about you, too. Sorry I won't be seeing you tonight.'

'You were going to see me?'

'Yeah, but I can't now 'cause of Mom and Dad. But I'll drop by tomorrow like always.'

'Good. I'll save you a seat on the glider.'

I smile. 'Love you, Granny.'

'Love you too, sweetheart.'

We hang up and for a second I feel happy. Then I open my closet. *Sigh.*

I text my cousin Madi: 'What you wearing?'

She doesn't answer. She's probably texting a million friends about the cool party last night I wasn't invited to. I hope her thumbs fall off.

I put on this stupid Junior Miss outfit Mom got me. It makes me look like I'm in kindergarten only taller. At least it's not one of Madi's. Everyone at school knows I wear her hand-me-downs, especially when she says stuff like, 'Was I ever that flat?'

Madi's my best friend except I hate her. When we were little, she decided what toys I could play with. Now she decides who I can have as friends, which is nobody except the cool kids at her table in the caf. And they're not even friends. They don't invite me to their parties and I have to laugh along when Madi throws shade about my hand-me-downs and where I live.

What kind of loser puts up with that?

A loser like me, that's who. I'm so like my parents it makes me puke. 'Cause for the record, Uncle Chad and Aunt Jess coming here isn't 'special'. It's *unbelievable*, as in seeing Martians at Burger King unbelievable. My parents pretend it's 'cause Uncle Chad's so busy with his tractor dealership and Aunt Jess with her social committees. But the *real* reason is we live in a one-storey aluminum box near the highway and they live where the houses are two-storey brick and the streets have sidewalks.

I mean, Aunt Jess doesn't even drop by for Mom to do

her hair. She and Madi go to Sylvie's over in Woodstock 'cause, 'Sylvie isn't a hairdresser: she's a stylist'. Also, she was born in Montreal and has this 'Je ne sais quoi', which is about all the French Aunt Jess knows.

Is Mom calling me?

'Zoe, for the last time, get out here. They're almost at the steps.'

I take my place at the door, five steps back from my parents. Dad's changed into the special herringbone suit he wears when he's asked to do the scripture reading. He pats the jacket pocket where he keeps Grampa's lucky watch.

The Mackenzies knock. Mom counts to ten before opening the door, so they won't know she's been hovering at the window.

'Jess, Chad, Madi!' Mom says, like this is a pleasant surprise.

Apparently the Mackenzies didn't get the memo about tonight being special. They're wearing what Aunt Jess calls 'leisure attire'. Oh yeah, and Madi's in jeans. Designer, but still. She takes one look at my Junior Miss outfit and her eyes go, *Please tell me I never wore that. Ever.*

Mom hugs Aunt Jess like she's her long-lost sister, which is sort of true.

'You didn't need to go to all this trouble,' Aunt Jess says, glancing at the nylon sheets on the hair dryers.

'No trouble,' Mom says, as if Aunt Jess meant it.

'Oh, and what have you done with your hair?'

Mom blushes. 'Just a little this and that.'

Uncle Chad hands Dad a bottle of wine. 'A little something for dinner.' By which he means *their* dinner, since my family doesn't drink. Except for me: apparently I'm this raging alcoholic for sneaking half a beer at Madi's two years ago. Which She Gave Me.

All the same, Dad takes it 'cause, hey, it's Uncle Chad and Aunt Jess. Mom offers them seats on the Hide-a-Bed; she and Dad sit on the sink chairs. This is when Madi and I used to go outside, only since high school she's allergic to being seen at our place – which, okay, so am I. Instead we go to my bedroom.

Madi closes the door and gives me a look. 'You're not going to get the money.'

2

I make a face: *Money? Hunh?*

Madi sighs like I'm simple. 'So your family can buy the old Tip Top Tailors? So your mom can move her salon to Main Street? That's why we're here. You know that, right?'

'Yeah.' I totally don't.

Madi rolls her eyes up into her head. I hope they stay there. 'You are *such* a bad liar. So, okay: your mom called my mom about us coming to dinner, and my mom said, "How about a restaurant?" 'Cause eating here? Really? But your mom said no, it had to be private, so she and your dad could ask *my* dad about a loan; and my mom was too embarrassed to say, "What, are you *kidding?*"'

Am I hearing this?

'Anyway,' Madi goes, 'my dad tells Mom, "If your dumb-ass sister and her idiot husband can't get a bank loan, they should put his mother in the county nursing home, move into *her* place, and sell their dump for cash."'

'Your father wants to put Granny Bird in Greenview Haven?'

'Well, she's hardly normal. Mom says she's demented.'

'Aunt Jess said that in front of you?'

'It's hardly a secret. Your grandmother's a garbage picker.'

'She is not. Granny collects things other people don't want.'

'Yeah. It's called garbage.'

'Quit it. There's nothing wrong with her.'

'To you, maybe. But ask our moms.'

'As if they're something special.'

'Well, *mine* is.'

'Only 'cause she married Uncle Chad. Granny's way more special than her.'

'Oh, she's special all right. Mom's *so* humiliated: "Why did Carrie have to marry into the Birds? If only she hadn't gotten in trouble." See, that's the difference between us. *My* parents wanted me.'

'So did mine.'

'Maybe that's what they tell you, but Mom knows different.' Madi checks her nails. 'Speaking of being unwanted, I was trying to find a nice way to say this, but there *is* no nice way, so I'm just going to say it: stop talking to me at school, stop sitting at my table, and don't visit my locker. Okay?'

I feel seasick. 'Madi?'

'Sorry if that sounds harsh, but everyone thinks you're a joke. Especially Katie and Caitlyn.'

'Katie and Caitlyn? They were nothing before they got tits.'

'Excuse! Me!' Madi says. 'They look up to me. So stay away.'

'But we go all the way back to when we were little.'

'Don't remind me.'

Why am I pleading? Stop it. Stop! 'And what about last summer when your cousin Danny came to visit from Saskatoon? Who hid your condoms? Who hid your hash? Me. In my old Barbie's Dream House box, right where you told me. And when Mom and Dad found them, who got yelled at and grounded and lost her phone for two months? And I didn't tell. Ever.'

'So what if you had? I'd have said you were lying and you'd have been in *more* trouble. You know it, too. Remember when we were on playdates and I'd pretend you hit me and your mom made you sit in the corner? Too funny.'

'You're so unfair.'

'It is what it is.'

'You only say that 'cause your dad says it and you think it sounds adult. Well, all it sounds like is, you're a big suckhole who thinks I should eat your shit.'

Madi smiles like she's Aunt Jess. 'You're so immature. Speaking of which, Ricky Saunders is totally out of your league, so quit dreaming.'

'Who said I'm into Ricky Saunders?'

'Come on. The way you look at him over at the jocks' table and drool when he comes by my locker with Dylan? Dylan's my boyfriend, you know: it's embarrassing. Gross.' She sits on my bed, pulls out her phone and texts.

'Get off my bed, Suckhole.'

Suckhole giggles. Apparently, some friend has said something hilarious. Yeah, I told her, she texts back.

'You think you can laugh about me in my own room?' I grab for her phone.

'Stay back or I scream.'

'Dinner,' Mom calls from down the hall.

We squish round the dinette set. Uncle Chad has a beer gut and Aunt Jess is 'well-upholstered' so it's hard to move my elbows. Dad says grace. I want to scream.

For the next half-hour, Madi's halo is so big I'm surprised her head doesn't cave in. She sits up straight like I'm supposed to, says please and thank you, and even eats her turnip. Meanwhile, Uncle Chad and Aunt Jess make small talk about his tractors and her running the Fall Fair Committee.

Mom and Dad don't say anything. They just nod like zombies on happy pills. I'll bet Uncle Chad's told them about the loan. After dessert, he pushes back his chair and pats his belly like it's a baby.

'That was some meal, Carrie.'

'Yes, it was just lovely, just lovely,' Aunt Jess says and glances at her watch. 'Why, look at the time.'

It's not even eight o'clock, but who wants to hang around a funeral? We head to the door. Aunt Jess is all, 'We really must do this more often,' and Mom and Dad are all, 'You betcha,' only it looks like they're trying not to vomit.

Uncle Chad squeezes Dad's shoulder. 'It is what it is.'

'Oh well, we'll find a way,' Dad says with his goofy shrug. 'Where there's a will there's a way, right?'

Uncle Chad shoots him a look like he's terminal. 'That's what they say.'

The door closes.

Mom pulls a Kleenex out of her sleeve. Dad takes off his shoes.

I put my hands on my hips. 'So when were you going to tell me?'

Mom daubs her eyes. 'What?'

'About Tip Top Tailors. About moving the salon. I mean, excuse me, aren't I part of the family?'

'You eavesdropped?' Mom says.

'As a matter of fact, Madi told me. She also said Granny's demented, Dad's an idiot and you're a dumb ass.'

'How dare you talk to us like that?'

'I'm quoting.'

'Don't tell tales about your cousin,' Dad says. 'Madi's well behaved.'

'Like Satan is well behaved.'

'Go to your room.'

'Not before you tell me what's going to happen to Granny.'

Dad squeezes his toes. 'Nothing's going to happen to Granny.'

'It better not.' I go to my room all tough, but inside I can hardly breathe.

3

Next day at school in the halls, Suckhole sails by with her BFFs, Katie and Caitlyn, aka the Suckhole-ettes. I picture them chased through the woods by psychos with chainsaws. I pass Ricky Saunders. We never talk 'cause he's in grade eleven and cool, but he always smiles at me. I used to pretend it meant something. Today I wonder if he knows about my crush and thinks it's funny. I look away.

At lunch, I stare straight ahead as I walk through the cafeteria. I pass Suckhole's table: they giggle. I act like I don't notice.

Is the whole caf staring me? What are they thinking? What are they saying?

I try to walk normal till I get to a table at the back. Emily Watkins is picking her nose and sticking it under her chair. 'What are you doing here?' she says like I'm lost.

'Eating. At least I was.'

Across the table, Eric, the school drug store, is drumming his knapsack: he's so stoned that when teachers call his name he thinks it's a trick question.

People are laughing. *Is it about me?* My chest and fingers prickle. I get up, stick out my chin like I don't care, toss my lunch in the garbage and hide in the girls' bathroom. The bell rings. I can't go to class. I run outside, grab my bike and head to Granny's.

Granny lives in a big, yellow-brick two-storey on a quarter-acre lot, with a widow's walk, a wrap-around verandah, and most of its shutters. Mom says it looks like a hobo house. Well, it's not Granny's fault that Dad's so clumsy. When he patched the roof, the shingles didn't match and tar went everywhere. When he painted the window frames, drips went over the brick. And he says the yard's too big to mow and water every week, so no surprise, it looks like crap.

If my parents hired people, things would be okay, only, 'We don't have the money'. Fine, then don't complain. At least Granny doesn't live in a cheesy beauty salon. Her place even has a name: the Bird House. Not because of the bird baths and feeders either. No, 'cause it's been in the Bird family since the 1920s. Granny and Grampa moved back to take care of my great-grandfather when Dad was seven.

I drop my bike inside the gate. Granny's on the verandah glider in her plaid dress and bulky black sweater. It's kind of her uniform, along with the red leather purse slung over her shoulder so she won't forget where she put it. It has her wallet, car keys, Kleenex, surprises, and a phone my parents got her in case she falls and can't get up.

Granny's eyes light up: 'Zoe! What's the magic word?'

I'm too old for this but it makes her happy. 'Rhubarb.'

'Pie!' Granny hugs me. 'Want to go inside?'

'Why? Don't you like it here?'

It's not Granny's fault, but her place smells of old person. On good days, the air is heavy-sweet, like the inside of a cookie jar. On other days, well, Granny doesn't clear the mousetraps. Dad replaces them when he comes by once a week with any mail he's picked up at Canada Post, which is basically nothing.

We rock together on the glider. When I was little, I'd crawl underneath and count the earwigs curled up in the screw holes.

'So,' Granny says, 'what does my little bird Bird have to tell me today?'

I want to make up fun stuff, but out of nowhere my head's on her shoulder and I'm going on about how Madi kicked me off her cafeteria table – where, okay, maybe I don't belong, but sitting there was the only thing halfway cool about me.

'You don't need Madi,' Granny says. 'Make other friends.'

'Who'd want me?'

'Anyone with a brain.'

'Why?' I sniffle.

'Because you're good, and kind, and loyal, and you have the biggest heart in the world.'

'You're just saying that.'

'Are you calling your granny a liar? Who else has a grandchild visit them every day? So you forget that little Madi toad. Those Mackenzies always think they're better than everyone. Well, want to know why her great-uncle had a closed casket? He passed out on the railroad tracks. Ended up in five pieces. They never did find the feet.'

I've heard that story a million times, but it always makes me laugh. 'What do you think happened to them?'

'I think a couple of dogs had a chew and died of foot poisoning.'

'Or Uncle Chad hid them in the freezer for a souvenir.'

'Or your aunt Jess made them into soup.'

'Or somebody kicked them up Madi's ass.'

Granny slaps her leg. 'Now you're talking.'

Granny and I look out at her yard. I love all the bird baths, especially after it rains and the robins and jays splash around. I also love the baby carriages and my old Tonka truck: she used to grow flowers in them, so really they're more like planters. Then there's the mannequin with the shower cap lounging in the wheelbarrow – we call him Fred – and the windmill from the old miniature golf club. Everything has a story, even the bird nests lining her verandah.

Today, there's something new. 'Where did that tricycle come from?'

Granny frowns. 'That's a mystery. What's your theory, Detective Bird?'

'Some kid left it?'

'I wonder where he went?'

'Maybe he was kidnapped in an ice-cream truck,' I wink. 'Let's check the Tastee Freeze. I'll bet we'll find him in a hot fudge sundae.'

Granny laughs, pats my knee and we get into her old Corolla. Her door won't shut tight 'cause it's dented in. Granny ties the front and rear window frames together with a dog collar.

'What happened to the door, Granny?'

'Some fellow must've backed into me in the parking lot.'

We drive off, ignoring the dinging sound. Granny's careful. She goes slow and when we get near parked cars, she steers into the middle of the road. Some guy honks behind us. Granny pulls to the curb and lets him pass. 'People today.' Her lips move like she's concentrating on a grocery list.

'Granny?'

She shushes me with her hand. 'I'm thinking . . . We're going somewhere.'

'Yes. To the Tastee Freeze.'

'Well, of *course* to the Tastee Freeze.' She taps her finger on the wheel.

'Two streets up, to the left?'

'I know that. Your granny's just a little distracted is all.'

At the Tastee Freeze, Granny stays in the car while I

order our sundaes. She watches me eat, then gives me hers. 'We should get going.'

'We just got here.'

'You can't trust people these days. When you're gone, they clean you out.'

As we pull into her drive, I think about how I imagine murderers in the closets when I come home and Mom and Dad are away. 'Want me to help search your place to make sure nobody's snuck in?'

'God bless you.'

Granny's place is cluttered like my bedroom, only with crusty antiques and things she keeps 'just because'. She checks the main floor while I do upstairs, starting with her bedroom. Not to be mean, but she *should* wash her sheets. Still, if you can't live like you want when you're old, when can you?

For fun, I look in her closets, armoires, and under the bed where she keeps scrapbooks and family photo albums. Her night table is full of framed pictures, too: of Grampa, me, Mom and Dad, and Uncle Teddy when he was little.

Uncle Teddy was twelve years older than Dad. He died before Granny and Grampa moved here to look after great-grandpa. Once, I asked Granny what happened. She teared up and left the room. Dad says to leave it alone, so it must have been awful, like maybe he killed himself? Anyway, I think he was her favourite 'cause the dust on his picture is smudged from her picking it up.

17

'All clear downstairs,' Granny calls.

'All clear up here,' I call back.

Outside, Granny leans against the verandah railing. 'When you're old, they want you gone.'

'I don't, Granny.'

'I know, Pumpkin.' She gives me a hug. I wish she'd never let go.

4

It's breakfast. Mom pokes her fork at Dad. 'Jess and Chad have a point. Think of that pile of cards by the stove. Your mother's place could go up anytime. People would say we should have done something.'

'It's not that bad,' Dad says. His shoes have been off since Sunday.

'Oh no? Those little blisters on your arches are back.'

'Hello,' I go, 'I'm eating.'

Mom ignores me. 'When was the last time you went through her fridge?'

'Carrie, I can't do that.'

'Why not? I'll bet half her groceries are rotten. What if she gets food poisoning?'

Dad closes his eyes like he's praying. 'I'll have a look before lunch.'

'No. *I'll* have a look. You say you'll look but you won't. And speaking of groceries, Heather Watkins saw her at the store in her dressing gown.'

That's a lie. Granny never wears anything except her plaid dress.

'Did you hear me, Tim? Heather Watkins saw your

19

mother at the store in her dressing gown!' Mom sees my death stare. 'What?'

'Nothing.'

'Don't give me that. Spit it out.'

'Mrs Watkins should stick her nose up her butt. And before she talks about Granny, she should stop Emily from sticking her snot on the cafeteria chairs.'

'That's enough, young lady.'

'You asked.'

Mom clatters the dishes to the sink. 'The truth is, since your grampa died your granny's been off the rails. Never mind. Ignore the obvious.'

'The obvious is, you want Granny locked up so you can grab her place and move your stupid salon to Main Street.'

Mom whirls round, hands full of cutlery.

'Go ahead. Stab me, why don't you?'

'Zoe. Carrie.' Dad says.

Mom starts to cry. I grab my backpack. As I stomp out the door, Dad says, 'Carrie, she didn't mean it.' But I did.

Forget school. If Mom's coming to Granny's, I have to clear her fridge. I drop my bike by the verandah, knock and step inside. 'Granny?'

No answer. She's normally up by now. Sometimes she naps on the comfy couch in the den, where Grampa slept when he couldn't climb the stairs. She's not there today, though, or in the living and dining rooms, either. I check the kitchen. *Woah what a death stench!*

I go upstairs and peek in her room. The curtains are closed. Granny's lying on her bed, fully dressed. I edge over slowly, so I don't trip on boxes or stub my toe on the garden gnome.

'Granny,' I whisper. 'It's Zoe.'

She sits bolt upright. 'Zoe, what are you doing here? It's past your bedtime.'

'It's nine in the morning.'

'My goodness.' Granny blinks. 'I have to tinkle.' She navigates to the bathroom. 'You can keep me company, if you like.'

'That's okay. Why don't you close the door?'

'I need to see where I am.'

I go down to the kitchen to solve the mystery of the death stench plus hide the cards by the stove. The mousetraps are empty. I squirt detergent down the sink drain to cover whatever's rotting, but it's not that. I check under the papers across from the sink. There's a dried up hamburger under some flyers, but it's not that, either. I toss it all in a big, green garbage bag and open the fridge.

Granny comes into the kitchen. 'Looking for something?'

'No. Granny, why don't you throw things out?'

'Waste food?' She squints at the counter by the stove. 'Didn't I have cards there?'

'I put them in a drawer.'

'Why?'

'Mom's coming over. She doesn't like to see stuff by the stove.'

'That's her problem. When things go in drawers, they disappear.'

'Granny, before we think about the cards, want to play a Detective Bird refrigerator game.'

'What is it?'

'Actually, it's *What Was It*? We point at things. If the other person can't figure out what it was, we throw it out. Like, this plastic bag with the green mush. What was it?'

'Beats me.'

'So out it goes.' I toss it in the bag.

'Wait. I might want that.'

'What for?'

'How should I know?'

'Fine. I'll put it back when Mom leaves.' Not. 'Now it's your turn. Pick something you don't know what it is.'

Granny points at a pan of soup with grey fuzz growing on it.

'This is Mom if she saw that.' I make a face.

Granny laughs and makes an even bigger face. We go back and forth until we're howling. Next thing you know, we're ditching mystery meat in puffed-up packages, old eggs, and lumpy milk. But even when we're down to the nasty ketchup bottles, there's still that smell.

We open cupboards. Nothing. Then I open the stove. There's a raw chicken in a roasting pan.

Granny claps her hands. 'I wondered where that went.'

A knock at the front door. 'Yoo-hoo.'

Mom!

'Tim, Carrie, what a surprise,' Granny says, heading to the door. 'Zoe didn't tell me you'd be joining us.'

'What's Zoe doing here? Holy Toledo, what's that smell?'

I toss the roasting pan into the garbage bag and try to haul it out the back door before they get here. The bottom bursts. There's crap everywhere.

Mom and Dad come into the kitchen. Dad's mouth bobs open and shut like a goldfish. Mom covers her nose with her arm. 'I'm going to be sick.'

'Toilet's down the hall,' Granny says.

'I'm going to be sick, I'm going to be sick.'

'I heard you the first time! Down the hall. Don't throw up in my kitchen.'

'Mom, Dad, just go outside. I'll clean it all up. Everything'll be fine.'

'It won't be fine!' Mom says. 'Tim, do something.'

'What?' Dad sweats.

'Yes, what?' Granny asks. 'What's going on?'

'You don't know?' Mom gasps.

'I know you're in my kitchen. What I don't know is why.'

'Mother—' Dad says.

'Don't "Mother" me,' Granny snaps. 'Zoe and I were having a visit. Next thing I know Missy Ferguson's going to vomit in my kitchen.'

Mom whirls on Dad. 'This can't go on.'

'What can't go on?' Granny goes.

'THIS!' Mom waves her arms. 'Who knows what's living in the walls, the furniture?'

'Mom,' I blurt, 'ever wonder what's living in your wig?'

'To the car!'

'Zoe's staying right here,' Granny says, steamed as a kettle. 'I invited *her*. Not *you*. It's you that needs to be going.'

Mom's eyes explode. 'Tim! Are you going to let her speak to me like that?'

Dad's melting. 'Mother. Please. Tell Carrie you're sorry.'

'Why?' Granny says. 'She's *your* problem, not mine. Get her out of here.'

'Yeah.' I stand beside Granny. 'Things were perfect before you got here.'

'Zoe—' Dad says.

'Well, they were. We cleared the cards. We cleaned out the fridge. We did lots of stuff. Then you guys came and everything went crazy.'

'Zoe, just – just—'

'Leave her alone!' Granny goes. 'You're dumb as cows and twice as homely.'

'We need to call someone!' Mom says.

Granny punches 911 on the wall phone. 'We need you out, is what we need. So leave or I'll have you arrested for trespassing.'

'Mother – for Heaven's sake, Mother—'

'Police? Yes, I . . . I . . .' Granny totters back and forth. Her face goes white. Her eyes go wide. The receiver falls out of her hand. She drops to the ground.

'Granny!'

She doesn't move. Mom grabs the receiver. 'Police. This is an emergency.'

I hold Granny's hand. 'Wake up, wake up.'

Dad flaps his arms. 'God! God! Help us, God!'

Next thing I know, Granny's in an ambulance, Dad and me beside her, Mom following in our car. We fly through the countryside to the county hospital, emergency entrance. The paramedics wheel Granny away.

5

I've been sitting opposite Mom and Dad in the waiting room for hours. No sound except a mother on the other side of the room going, 'Stop that. Stop that,' while her kid runs around pretending he's a race car.

Dad leans over to undo his shoelaces.

'We're in public,' Mom whispers.

He grabs his armrests like on that plane to Mexico. Mom clicks her nails. My eyes drill holes through their skulls: *This is your fault. If Granny dies—* No, please God, don't let Granny die. If You let her live, I'll believe in You for ever.

A doctor comes through the swinging doors. 'I'm looking for the Birds.' We huddle round him and shake hands. 'I'm Dr Milne.'

'Is Granny all right? What's happening? How is she?'

Dr Milne smiles at me the way Dad used to. 'Your Granny's fine. She's awake, talking, able to move. She's been asking for you.' He looks to Mom and Dad. 'There's bruising, but no broken bones. We've put her on a fluid drip. She was very dehydrated. That's likely why she fell. Everything should be fine, but we'd like to keep her overnight for observation.'

'Certainly.'

We follow Dr Milne through the swinging doors and down a corridor to Granny's room. She's propped up in a bed at the far end. Her arms poke out of her hospital gown like reeds. My parents talk with the doctor while I run inside and give her a kiss. 'Granny!'

'Zoe! What's the magic word?'

'Rhubarb.'

'Pie.' She laughs. 'They tell me I had a fall.'

I nod. 'How do you feel?'

'How do you think? Say, what's this thing sticking into my arm?'

'A drip tube. The doctor says you were dehydrated.'

'Oh.' Granny blinks. 'You know, I had the strangest dream. I was planting tulip bulbs with Teddy. He put the bulbs in the earth and I covered them, and he said, "Are they dead?" and I said, "Why?" and he said, "Because we buried them. Should we pray?" So we did, and then I said, "In the spring, they'll be born again as flowers." He hugged me and said, "I want to be a flower." Then I woke up and there was a doctor and nurses and now here you are, and isn't that the strangest thing?'

I nod. *What's keeping Mom and Dad so long?*

Granny strokes my cheek. 'Your uncle Teddy was like you when he was a boy. Such a good heart.'

My parents come in with Dr Milne.

'Tim, Carrie, what a lovely surprise,' Granny says.

27

'Mother,' Dad shuffles, 'the doctor would like to ask you a few questions.'

'What kind of questions?'

'Just a few questions to see how you are,' Dr Milne says. He sits on the chair across the bed from me, puts his clipboard on his knee and takes out a pen.

'Zoe,' Mom says, 'maybe you'd like to wait for us in the hall.'

Granny squeezes my hand. 'If there's to be any questions, Zoe stays right where she is. She's my witness.'

'Why do you need a witness?' Mom asks.

'As if you don't know.'

Dr Milne signals my parents. 'It's fine.'

Granny tosses Mom a *So There* look. 'So, Doctor, what can I do for you?'

'I was wondering if you could tell me what day it is?'

Granny's eyes narrow. 'Why, it's today.'

'And what day is that?'

'The same day it was when I woke up.'

Dr Milne makes a note. 'Can you tell me what season it is?'

Granny glances out the window: 'Well, I don't see any snow, so I guess it isn't winter. How about summer?'

'It's fall, Mother,' Dad says.

'You think I don't know that?'

'Mrs Bird,' Dr Milne asks pleasantly, 'could you please

count backwards from a hundred by nines for me? One hundred, ninety-one, eighty-two and so forth?'

'Of course I can.' She stares at him.

'Well then, would you, please?'

'Why? It's plain foolish.'

Dr Milne makes a note. 'Instead of questions, let's play a game. I'll give you three words, we'll talk and then I'll ask you for the words.'

Granny gives him an eyebrow. 'You get paid to do this?'

'An easy life, hunh?' Dr Milne jokes; Granny grips my hand harder. 'Now the three words I want you to remember are: Boy, box, pencil. All right?'

'Boy, box, pencil.' Granny repeats over and over under her breath.

'So,' Dr Milne says casually, 'I had a good breakfast today: eggs, toast and coffee. What did you have?'

'Boy box pencil – the same – boy box pencil.'

'Your fall must've surprised you.'

Granny nods, her lips going *boy box pencil boy box pencil.*

Dr Milne suddenly points out the window. 'Is that a deer?'

'What?' Granny turns her head. 'A deer? Where?'

'By the bushes.'

'Which bushes?'

'Darn, it's run off,' Dr Milne says. 'So, Mrs Bird, could you please tell me the three words.'

Granny glares at him. 'Boy, box . . . boy, box . . . boy, box and the other one.'

'Good. And the other one?'

'Why should I tell you?'

'Mother,' Dad goes. 'You don't know, do you?'

'Don't tell me what I know and what I don't know. You don't know nothing, Mister Know Nothing.'

'Then tell the doctor the three words.'

'BOY, BOX, PENCIL,' I yell. 'STOP BEING SO MEAN!'

'You tell 'em, Zoe! Boy, box, penicillin!' Granny bangs her fist on the bed rail. 'You think I don't know what these questions are about? You think I've lost it. You think I've gone loony. Hah! Where's my car? I'm getting out of here.'

'She drives?' Dr Milne asks.

'Yes, *she* drives,' Granny spits. 'How do you think *she* got here?'

Dr Milne looks to my parents. 'Perhaps we should move to the hall.'

'Perhaps you should go to hell!' Granny yells as he leads them out. 'Don't think you can talk about me behind my back.' She goes to get out of bed.

'Granny, the tube. You'll hurt yourself. Don't worry. I'm here. It's okay.'

'It's not okay. They want to put me away.'

'No. The doctor just wants you to stay overnight. They want to make sure you've recovered.'

'Oh, do they now?'

'Yes. Please, Granny. Trust me. Stay for tonight. That's all. Tomorrow you'll be back home and we'll sit on the verandah and laugh.'

Her eyes are scared. 'I'd rather be dead than trapped in Greenview Haven.'

"That's not going to happen. I won't let it. Not ever.'

'Promise?' she pleads.

'Yes. Promise.'

6

We cross the parking lot. Dad has Granny's purse and her clothes in a bag for washing. 'What you did back there was a disgrace.'

'I was standing up for Granny is all.'

'They could hear you screaming all the way down the corridor,' Mom says. 'I've never been so embarrassed in all my life.'

What else is new?

We pile into the car and Dad starts the engine. As we pull onto the highway, Mom fans herself with the map from the glove compartment. It's quite the show, 'cause yeah, the day's been all about *her*. I want to kick the back of her seat so hard she'll fly through the windshield.

'You're not the only one who loves Granny,' Dad says. 'For Pete's sake, she's my mother. I've been responsible for her and your grampa before that – and it hasn't been a picnic, let me tell you.'

'So?'

'Zoe, we're not the enemy. We only want what's best for her. I hardly sleep. You've no idea all there is to stress about.'

'This morning you told Mom things weren't that bad.'

'And look what's happened since then.'

'What's happened is you barged in looking for trouble.'

Mom swings round and shakes the map in my face. 'If you used your head, you'd be worried sick about your granny having fires, heart attacks, strokes—'

'She has a phone.'

'Much good it did today,' Mom snaps. 'And what if she wanders? Mrs Glover froze to death last winter.'

'Granny's cell phone has a GPS. It's in her purse. She wears it all the time, even in bed.'

'Forget emergencies,' Dad says. 'What about her diet? Her hygiene?'

'We can look after that.'

'Oh, really? I'd like to see you try and give her a bath.'

'I could if I had to. Better that than Greenview Haven.'

'If only it were that simple.' Mom pulls out her phone. 'Jess, Carrie here. We've been at the hospital. Tim's mother collapsed . . . No, she'll be fine, whatever "fine" means. She's skin and bones. And who knows when she did her toenails last. They're so long they curl right under her toes. It was so embarrassing. Thank God the nurses are going to clip them . . . Well, of course she's not in her head, but the doctor says we can't place her unless she's a danger.'

Hooray!

'Yes, I know, it's crazy, totally crazy. I've been dealing with crazy all day,' Mom says. 'At least he pulled her driver's licence.'

I grab the back of Mom's seat. 'He took Granny's licence? How will she get around?'

'Enough!' Dad's like he's ready to plough us into the ditch.

'Granny's safe! She drives slow!'

'I said, enough!' Dad yells.

'Anywho,' Mom says sweetly, 'the county's sending someone in the next few days to check that her place is senior-friendly. I need to spruce things up or they'll think we don't care, and we do. If I had a nickel for every time I tried to clean and got my head chewed off I'd be millionaire. You'd think her dust and dirt were heirlooms. Please, *please*, could you give me a hand? I'm too embarrassed to ask anyone else.'

I'll bet Aunt Jess is doing cartwheels. She loves being shocked as much as Mom. It's their favourite hobby.

'Thanks,' Mom says. 'See you in a jiffy.' She hangs up.

'I'll help too,' I say. 'I know where everything goes.'

Mom snorts. 'You'd make a bigger mess than we started with.'

'Cow.'

'What did you say?'

'Cow. I'm looking at the cow in that field, do you mind?'

Apparently she does.

Back home, Mom tosses Granny's skirt and sweater in the wash and her underwear in the trash, then grabs some garbage bags, cleaning stuff, and a bottle of hand sanitizer and heads out to meet Aunt Jess.

Dad takes Granny's car keys out of her purse and puts them in the old cufflinks box in his bottom dresser drawer. 'Whew boy.' He turns on the TV, sits at one of the sink chairs, and dries his sweaty feet with a hair dryer.

Whew boy: No kidding.

Mom phones at six to say she won't be home for dinner; Dad and I have leftover meatloaf. She drags herself through the door at nine: 'They should put me on a stained-glass window. I stink like the Bird House.'

Mom goes to the bedroom to get ready for a shower. Dad follows her. I look at her counter of hair sprays. *She* talks about stink? I eavesdrop from outside their door.

'The filth, the clutter. We worked so hard and it hardly made a dent,' Mom says. 'How can she live like that? How is that not a danger?'

'Carrie, what are we going to do? What are we going to do?'

Mind your own business, that's what. Who cares if Granny's old and different. At least she's free.

7

Next day before class, I'm getting stuff out of my locker, when—

'Bird Turd.'

I whirl round. The hall's packed; I can't tell who said it. I hear it again between math and science. At lunch, I speed-walk to the back of the caf and sit with my back to the world. My favourite girl band, Suckhole and the Suckhole-ettes, come over.

'We just want to say we're here for you,' Suckhole says.

'Yeah,' from Katie, 'if I were you, I'd be freaking out.'

'Hunh?'

'Your grandmother,' Suckhole whispers solemnly.

'Granny's fine. She had a fall, that's all.'

Suckhole takes my hand like she's a nurse or something. 'We know she's okay as in she didn't break anything. But her mind. Aunt Carrie says it's like the furniture's gone and she's down to the wallpaper.'

'What?' I yank my hand away.

'Come on. She couldn't tell the doctor what day it was. She didn't even know the season.'

'She did too. He asked stupid questions. Granny tossed it back.'

'Don't be mad,' Katie says. 'It's not like we're judging.'

'No, we're not judgey at all,' from Caitlyn. 'You being mental makes sense now. You're stressed. I mean, we've seen the Bird House, but the other stuff!'

'Don't be ashamed,' Suckhole says. 'It is what it is.'

I pull my hand away. 'Granny's fine. I see her every day.'

'Then you know about the hole in the back of her comfy couch. Aunt Carrie thinks there's a squirrel living inside.' She takes a heavy breath. 'And you'll know about the pee stains.'

'There aren't any pee stains.'

Suckhole bites her lip. 'Well, all I can say is, don't sit on the chairs in the dining room. Mom said, "She must have run out of Depends, poor thing."'

'Stop making stuff up.'

'Our moms scrubbed two cans of Ajax in the toilets: the streaks at the bottom *still* wouldn't come out. They also had to throw away her carpet runner and half the rugs 'cause they were too gross to send to the cleaners. Seriously, they were so scared of disease and fungus, they had to wear oven mitts.'

'If Aunt Jess told you that, she's a liar!'

'Mom didn't tell me anything,' Suckhole says. 'I was there. I saw.'

'You were at Granny's?'

37

'I came over to help after school. I went through her drawers. I had to ditch her underwear. Ew.'

'When Madi was clearing your grandmother's crap, where were *you*?' from Katie.

'She was at home,' Suckhole goes. 'Aunt Carrie didn't want her there.'

I jump up. 'Shut your hole!'

'Zoe, people are watching,' Caitlyn says.

'Who cares?' I pound the table with both fists: 'I love Granny.'

'Really?' Caitlyn says. 'Madi does all the work and you do nothing.'

'Eat shit and die.' I stomp out of the caf with a toss to the tables: 'What are you butt-nuggets staring at?'

8

When I get to Granny's, my insides fall out. Her Corolla's at the end of the drive; the For Sale sign in the window has our phone number. Granny's sitting behind the wheel, staring straight ahead. She's in her plaid dress and black sweater, cleaned, her red purse slung over her shoulder.

I hop off my bike and into the passenger seat. 'Granny.'

Her face lights up. 'Zoe! What's the magic word?'

'Rhubarb.'

'Pie.' Granny beams.

'What are you doing out here in the car, Granny?'

'I don't know. I must have been going somewhere. It's a good thing you came when you did or you'd have missed me.' She goes to take her car keys out of the ignition. 'What happened to my keys?'

'You probably left them on the front vestibule,' I lie.

'Well, isn't that a stupid thing.' Granny gets out of the car and leads me towards the house. 'You know, Zoe, all day I've had the strangest notion that I've been at the hospital. It feels so real, but here I am.'

'You had a fall. They kept you at the hospital overnight. Mom and Dad brought you back this morning.'

Granny lets out a sigh of relief. 'So I haven't gone crackers after all.' She opens the door and we step inside. Granny freezes. 'Where's the carpet?'

'I think Mom sent some rugs out for cleaning.'

'Well, she'd better bring them back. People take things, they never come back.' She sticks her head in the den. 'Something's wrong.' She looks up the stairs. 'It's wrong.' She runs into the living room and grips the back of the piano. 'Floors. Why am I seeing floors? Who stole my rugs?'

'It's okay, Granny. Mom's just moved things around.'

'Where? How am I supposed to find anything?' Her hand flutters to her chest. 'I have to get out of here. I need air. I can't breathe.'

I follow her to the verandah. We rock on the glider till she calms down.

'Zoe,' she says, 'can I ask you something? Just between the two of us?'

'Sure.'

Granny looks over her shoulder like people are eavesdropping. 'Are your parents spying on me?'

'Why would they do that?'

'To know what I do. Where I go. They want an excuse to put me away. To steal my place. You'd tell me if they were spying, right?'

'Sure.'

Granny thinks a bit. 'Can I ask you something else?'

'Anything. Always.'

'The truth, now.' She stops the glider. 'Am I losing it?'

If anyone else asked if Granny was losing it, I'd say, *Don't be stupid*. Only this is Granny asking. I stare at my feet. 'That's a strange question.'

'So I am.'

'Just sometimes, Granny. And so what? I forget, too. Forgetting's normal.'

'I hope so.'

'Besides, you're older. You have so much more to remember.'

Granny tries to smile. 'I do, don't I? When I tilt my head, memories fall out my ears.' We listen to a blue jay. 'Zoe, there are times like now, when I know what's what. But between you and me, this morning's a dream and I'm afraid how I'll be tonight.'

'This morning doesn't count. You were at the hospital.'

Granny looks off. 'Your grampa and I came here to look after his father. Then I looked after *him*. Now it's my turn and there's no one.' She smooths her dress. 'Oh well. Guess I just have to put on my Big Girl pants.'

'*I'm* here for you, Granny,' I say in a small voice.

'Yes, you are. You're just like Teddy.'

'You said that yesterday.'

'Did I?'

'You never talk about him. Now you've said his name two days in a row.'

'I guess I have,' Granny says. 'I think about him more

and more. Isn't that strange? The older you get, the more you think about the past. Why is that?'

''Cause every day there's more past to think about?'

Granny chuckles. 'You.' She looks over the yard. 'Your Grampa and I brought Teddy and your dad here every summer to visit your great-grandparents.'

'Were there elves in the drain spout back then?' I grin.

'Oh, yes,' Granny grins back. 'Elves have been leaving candies in that drain spout since for ever. Teddy had china elves he played with, too. Your grampa was so mad when I got them.'

'Did Dad play with the elves?'

Granny rolls her eyes. 'Just once. He thought they could fly. Teddy was upset, but your dad was only two, so he forgave him. Anyway, by then, Teddy was a teenager: out of elves and into knitting.'

'What did Grampa say about *that*?'

'What *didn't* he say? I told him to zip it: If more men knit, the world would be less tangled.' Granny's face melts like butter. 'Teddy made the most beautiful sweaters, gloves, winter socks. He stitched us a pair of matching scarves once, yellow and orange with bursts of purple – they went all the way down to our knees. Teddy. If he was around, he'd protect me. But he's gone.' Her lips move as if she's talking to someone.

'Granny,' I whisper, 'want me to make you a sandwich?' She nods, but not like she's here.

I go inside. Mom and Aunt Jess have stocked the fridge and put fresh sheets on Granny's bed. There are boxes of Depends by her dresser and a drawer full of new panties and old-people socks. The bathrooms are cleaner, too. Good. A little help's all Granny needs.

All of a sudden I know what to do.

9

Back home, I concentrate on being polite. I set the table without being asked. I close my eyes when Dad says grace. Instead of grabbing stuff, I ask: 'Could you please pass me the casserole?'

Mom looks at me weird. 'Certainly.' She hands it to me.

'Thank you.'

'So . . .' she says, 'you were at Granny's today?'

'Yes,' I answer nicely.

Mom rearranges her bum like a hen on eggs. 'Maybe from now on, you could wait until after school? I've been getting calls from the attendance secretary.'

'Okay. Sorry.' I smile and chew. And chew. And chew.

My folks frown like they're trying to figure why I'm so polite. The eyes of the kitchen owl clock go back and forth between us.

I finally swallow. 'You and Aunt Jess really worked hard at Granny's. The bathrooms and kitchen look amazing.'

'Why, uh, thank you. It's a start anyway.'

'Madi says she cleaned out Granny's underwear drawer.'

Mom's eyes flicker. 'It was Aunt Jess's idea. I had no idea she'd be there.'

'Oh, I don't mind. Anything for Granny.'

Mom sits back. For the first time in ages, Dad actually breathes.

Time for my pitch: 'I know I've been a problem for you guys. I've made things way more stressful than they need to be, which isn't fair, especially knowing about your rashes and alopecia and whatnot. So I'd like to say I'm sorry and I have an idea for making life easier.'

'Oh?' from Mom. 'We're all ears,' from Dad. They lean forward for the Miracle at the Dinner Table.

I take a deep breath. 'I was thinking: what if I moved in with Granny? I can bring her meals from here and sleep in one of the guest rooms. That way you won't have to worry about her, and I'll be out of your hair.'

They stare at me like a couple of pithed frogs. Dad shifts in his chair. The vinyl seat makes a fart sound. 'That's a very interesting idea. Very original. Very . . .'

'Very considerate,' Mom says. 'But, honey, I'm afraid your granny's situation is more complicated than that. What happens when you're at school and she's alone? Or if she lights the stove in the middle of the night and there's a fire with you sleeping upstairs?'

'That's not going to happen.'

'How do you know? And think of all the temptations you'd have.'

'Meaning?'

'You know,' Mom says. 'The Dream House box?'

'That stuff wasn't mine.'

'Either way, we're responsible. Think what people would say.'

'Nothing worse than they say already.'

'The answer is no.'

There is the longest – but I mean *longest* – silence. Dad looks like he's not sure if he should keep breathing.

I doodle my casserole with my fork, slow and steady. 'Is it true I'm like Uncle Teddy?'

Dad goes grey. 'Where did that come from?'

'Granny. She's said it twice now. So am I?'

'No,' Mom says.

'How would you know? He died before Dad moved here.' I look back at Dad. '*Am* I?'

'Don't be rude to your mother.'

'Granny says he would've looked after her,' I say. 'She says he'd never have put her in a nursing home.'

'Who knows what he'd have done,' Dad says.

I squeeze my fork. 'How did he die?'

'What?'

'Uncle Teddy. How did he die? Did he kill himself?'

'Why would you think that?' Mom exclaims.

'Because you never say. All I can think is, it must have been awful, and what's more awful than that. So did he?'

Pause. 'Not exactly,' Dad says.

'What do you mean *not exactly*?'

'What I said.'

'Look, he did or he didn't. Yes or no?'

Dad tosses his napkin on the table and leaves the room. Mom shoots me a look and clears the dishes.

I throw up my hands. 'What did *I* do?'

'As if you don't know.' Mom leaves the room, too.

'All I know is, Granny said Uncle Teddy and I were the same.' I stand up and call after them: 'Why don't I know how he died?'

Uncle Teddy, you're like what's in the attic. Out of sight, but still around. What happened? How did you die?

10

Next day, the thought of the caf makes me sick, so I eat in the parking lot. Eric's splatto on the pavement like he's OD'd or something.

Maybe that's how Uncle Teddy died. Is it why my folks freaked out last summer?

In the photo on Granny's night table, Uncle Teddy and I have the same curly hair, but our eyes are different. His are guarded: mine bug out like Mrs Potato Head's.

My phone rings.

'Zoe, come quick, there's a thief in the house.'

'Relax, Granny, Mom and Aunt Jess just moved stuff. I'll be over after school.'

'No, now!' Granny exclaims. 'I came in from out back, heard noises upstairs, and grabbed a butcher's knife. He was in my bedroom. I have him cornered in the closet!'

I hear sirens. 'I'm on my way.'

By the time I get there, two cops have a weasely guy I've never seen by the maple tree. Neighbours huddle in clumps on the sidewalk. I drop my bike and run up the verandah steps.

'Stop!' one of the cops calls after me.

'My Granny's in there.' I zip inside. 'Granny?'

'Zoe,' she hollers from the den. 'Thank God you're here.'

Three other cops have boxed her in by the comfy couch.

'Who are you?' from the hairy cop.

'Zoe Bird. This is my granny. She called me about a robbery.'

'You tell 'em,' Granny says. 'They won't listen. You'd think *I* was the thief.'

'We found your grandmother holding a county case-worker hostage,' says the cop with the big ears.

'Hunh?'

'The caseworker found the door open. When no one answered, he went inside to make sure your grandmother was all right. He ended up in the bedroom. Your grand-mother blocked his exit with a butcher's knife. He phoned from a closet.'

'Apparently, if you're old, you can't defend yourself,' Granny snaps. 'Apparently, strangers can barge in, steal your things, God knows what all.'

'Granny's missing a few rugs,' I explain. 'She's worried about thieves.'

'Mr Weldon identified himself,' the woman cop says.

'So? Would you believe a stranger you found in your bedroom?'

Dad runs in on overdrive, Mom behind. 'Officers. Tim

Bird, her son. Carrie, my wife.' He sees me. 'Zoe? What are you—? No. Shut it. Just shut it.' He whirls on Granny. 'Mother, how could you?'

'How could I what?' Granny asks.

'You threatened a case worker with a butcher's knife!'

'Says who?'

'What happens now?' Mom asks the cops.

'Mr Weldon doesn't want to place charges,' says Big Ears, 'but this is a serious incident. We don't want anyone getting hurt. Can she be supervised?'

'*She* doesn't need to be supervised,' Granny pipes up. '*She's* not a child.'

Mom ignores her. 'No. We both work.'

Dad sticks his finger under his shirt collar. 'Perhaps we could discuss things across the hall?' The cops nod. 'Zoe, stay here with your grandmother.'

'We're not staying anywhere,' Granny says. 'We're going to the verandah. When we come back in, you better not be here.' She marches us outside. 'Get off my sidewalk,' she yells at the neighbours and sits on the glider.

I go to the railing and bring her the bird's nest with the tinfoil. 'Remember when you got this?'

She calms right down, eyes lit up. 'Tell me.'

'Dad was clearing round the top of your drain spout. There were babies in it. You put it on your window ledge and the mother found it. We watched her feed them until they could fly.'

50

Granny strokes the nest. 'What do you suppose happened to them?'

'I figure they're at your feeders with their children and grandchildren.'

'Granny birds,' Granny chuckles. We make up stories about the birds, and the whole world disappears, until my parents come out with the cops.

'Tim. Carrie.' Granny blinks. 'What are police doing here?'

'They've been looking for those people taking your things,' Dad says.

'About time.'

'We have all the evidence we need, Mrs Bird,' the woman cop says.

'Thank Heavens.' Granny shakes the cops' hands, they take off, and the neighbours start to go home.

'So, Mother,' Dad says, 'want to come to our place for something to eat?'

'I'm fine thanks. I had a big breakfast.'

'It's Sunday dinner,' Dad lies. 'You don't want to disappoint Zoe, do you?'

'All right, then. For Zoe.' Granny winks at me.

I wink back: I'll bet she hasn't eaten all day.

On our way to the car, Mom leans in to my ear, 'You need to be back at school.'

Granny overhears. 'Don't be daft. There's no school on Sunday. Zoe, hop in the car.'

'She has her bike,' Mom says.

'I'll pick it up later,' I go, all cheery.

Dad opens the passenger door for Granny. I join Mom in the backseat.

At the corner, we normally turn up to Main Street. Today we keep going. *Hunh?* We pull left at Malcolm, then right, and drive along the cemetery. *No!*

I stay calm for Granny. 'You're not going where I think, are you?'

Dad acts like I'm not here. 'Mother, have a look at all those rosehips. The cemetery's so well-tended.'

'Are we visiting your father?' Granny asks. 'We should stop for flowers.'

'Not today,' Dad says. 'We're just having a drive.'

No, we're not. What do I say? What do I do? We pass the cemetery gates. At the end of the road – Greenview Haven. 'Mom, Dad, please no.'

'Zoe, for everyone's sake – everyone's – don't make a scene,' Mom says.

Dad turns to Granny. 'I think the leaves are about to turn. Won't that be beautiful, Mother?'

My throat's like sandpaper. 'This isn't right.'

'We called Dr Milne,' Mom says to me. 'He's signed and faxed the papers. It's done.'

'What's done?' Granny asks.

Dad turns on the radio. 'Let's listen to some music.'

'I said, "*What's* done?" Turn off that noise.'

'Please, Dad . . .'

We pull into the parking lot, swing around the circular drive. A woman and two care workers are waiting. Dad hops out as the woman opens Granny's door.

'Mrs Bird, how lovely to meet you. I'm Gloria Beckwith.' She shakes Granny's hand, drawing her out of the car.

'Granny! Stay inside. It's a trap.' I fumble at my door; Dad's turned on the safety lock. I try scrambling over the seat to the front. 'It's Greenview, Granny!'

Mom grabs at me. 'Stop it, Zoe. It's for the best.'

Granny registers where she is. 'Greenview!' She tries to back up, but the men are behind her. They hold her above the elbows. 'Zoe! Help!'

'I can't! There's too many of them!'

Granny kicks at the men's legs. 'Where's Teddy? I want Teddy!'

'Teddy's gone, Mother,' Dad says. 'You'll love it here.'

The men drag her towards the glass doors. They slide open.

'Teddy won't let this happen. Teddy! Zoe! Teddy!'

Granny disappears into the nursing home.

11

By the time Dad comes back to the car, I'm howled out. He and Mom tear into me as we drive out of the parking lot. I hardly hear them. My head's full of Granny crying, struggling: *Everything she's been afraid of's come true. I promised it wouldn't. I failed. Will she blame me? Forgive me?*

'That scene you made,' Mom goes. 'I can't imagine what Mrs Beckwith must be thinking.'

Who cares?

'We tried so hard to move her in smoothly. It didn't have to be like that.'

It didn't have to be at all.

'Are you listening to a word I'm saying?'

'No.'

Dad slams on the brakes. He drops his head on the steering wheel. 'Zoe. We never wanted this.'

'You did too. You set her up. Someone should've been at her place when that guy came.'

'We had work to do,' Mom says.

'You'd have done it for Uncle Chad and Aunt Jess.'

'That's not true.'

'It is. But who cares anyway: you could've sent *me*.'

'You had school,' Dad says.

'Math's more important than Granny? Besides, you didn't have to bring her here. You could have taken her to our place.'

'There's barely room for the three of us,' Mom says. 'And what about the salon? She'd be sticking her nose in, repeating, blurting who knows what. My gals would be so uncomfortable.'

'They're more important than Granny?'

'No, but without them, how do we pay the bills?'

'Aside from that,' Dad says, 'what if your granny woke up one night and decided to go to the Bird House? You think she'd remember how? Streets are different in the dark. Who knows what could happen?'

'And how would we deal with her garbage-picking,' Mom adds. 'You want that stuff on our lawn, in our house?'

'It's no worse than your stupid hair dryers, your stupid neon sign, your stupid owl clock.'

Mom bites her tongue. We have a staring contest.

'Whew boy.' Dad takes ten deep breaths and starts to drive again. We're home in a couple of minutes.

'I can't wait till you're old,' I mutter as we go inside. 'I'll lock you in Greenview so fast your heads'll spin. When you cry and scream like Granny, I'll laugh.'

Mom's face crumples up. 'Go to your room.'

'Great. I don't want to see you anyway.'

'And no lunch.'

'Double great. I'm not hungry.'

Next morning: Saturday.

Mom and Dad leave at eight o'clock to move some of Granny's stuff to Greenview so she'll feel more at home. I have to stay here 'cause they don't want a repeat of yesterday. And if there ever *is* a repeat of yesterday, I won't get to see Granny again, period.

But even though I don't see her, I hear from her lots. The first call comes right after my folks are gone.

'Zoe, strangers woke me up. They said they'd bring me to breakfast. I scared them off, but they may be back. I don't know where I am. You have to find me.'

'Stay calm, Granny. You're at Greenview Haven.'

'The county home?'

'Yes.'

'What am I doing here? I have to get back to my place. People will be breaking in. They'll be taking my things.'

'Mom and Dad will be there soon. You can tell them all about it.'

'Thank God.'

Second call. Eight thirty-five.

'Zoe, I'm in this strange bedroom. Outside the window there's a parking lot. On the far side I think I can see the cemetery. Something isn't right.'

'Mom and Dad are on their way.'

'They better be. There's a crazy man down the hall yelling, "Help me! Help me!" I've pushed the chest of drawers against the door.'

'Move it back, Granny. If you don't, they'll think you've lost it.'

'Who?'

'The staff at Greenview.'

'Greenview? I'm at Greenview?'

'Yes.'

'Why wasn't I informed?'

'Dad must have forgotten. He's coming now.'

'I'm not sticking around here for your father. Where's my car?'

'At home.'

'Maybe I should call a taxi.'

'No, Granny. Wait for Dad.'

Third call. Eight fifty-five.

'Zoe, I'm in this room—'

'I know. Do you have a pen in your purse?'

'I'll see . . . Zoe, someone's been in my purse. They've stolen my car keys.'

'Don't worry, they're safe.'

'Where are they?'

'I'll explain later. Right now, just look for a pen.'

'Okay. I have a pen. Now what?'

'Write on the back of your hand: "Tim is coming".'

'Your dad is coming?'

'Yes. Write it on your hand. "Tim is coming".'

'"Tim is coming". Done.'

'Terrific. Next time you reach for your phone, read your hand.'

'"Tim is coming."'

'That's right.'

'What a relief. I don't know what I'd do without you. I love you, Pumpkin.'

'I love you too.'

Things stay good for an hour. Then:

'Zoe.' There's piano music and singing in the background. 'I was in this room. Your parents started bringing things in from my place. I told them to take them back home. They said *this* is my home. What's going on?'

'Let me speak to Dad.'

'He's not here.'

'Where is he?'

'How should I know?'

'So where are *you*?'

'I don't know. Wherever it is, it's full of couches and old people. Good Lord!'

'What?'

'I think that's Doctor Rutherford across the room. You watch out for Dr Rutherford. No matter what you go in for, he'll check your lady bits. Have a cough? He'll check your lady bits. Have the flu? He'll check your lady bits.'

'Granny, Doctor Rutherford retired when I was little.'

'He's a devil. And what's he doing with Mona Peasley?'

'Who?'

'Fred Peasley's widow. He was the undertaker. They caught him stuffing cadavers with newspapers. I thought they put Mona in the county home.'

'Granny, sit tight. I'm calling Dad. Soon as I know what's up I'll call back.'

'Good. There's a woman coming by with a cart of cookies and orange juice.'

'Talk to you in a minute.'

I hang up and speed-dial Dad: he picks up. 'Dad, where *are* you guys?'

'In Granny's room. We're unpacking.'

'She's scared. One of you needs to sit with her.'

'We can't right now. Too much to do.'

'Then I'm coming over.'

'Zoe, if you want to be on the visitors' list, stay where you are. A very nice nurse is keeping an eye on her. Do your homework. I have to go.'

I call Granny back: 'It's me. Zoe.'

'Zoe, I'm losing my mind. I'm in this room with people I haven't seen in years. I thought they were dead.'

'I'll be there tomorrow.'

'I need you now.'

'I'm stuck in bed,' I lie. 'I've been throwing up all day.'

'Oh my. You better take care of yourself.'

'I will. First, get your pen. I want you to write on your hand.'

'I already have something on my hand: "Tim is coming".'

'Stroke out "Tim" and write in "Zoe". Then add "tomorrow". Okay?'

'Okay . . . "Zoe is coming tomorrow". Good. I feel better already.'

12

When Mom and Dad get back, I'm spinning on a sink chair listening to my music. I close my eyes and nod to the beat as if they're not here.

'Granny has a lovely room,' Mom says. 'We've made it so homey.'

'The family pictures are by her bed just like at the Bird House,' Dad adds. 'And she's got her lamp and two paintings from the living room. We even brought the garden gnome.'

I keep bobbing my head, eyes closed.

'Honey,' Mommy says in her tired voice. 'We know you can hear us.'

I toss her a glance: *You want a gold star?*

'We've been working ourselves sick for Granny.'

'You locked her up.'

'It's not like that at all,' Dad says. 'We can bring her out for dinners and overnights. She just can't live unsupervised.'

'Like I said, she's a prisoner.'

'A *resident*. In a home where she'll be properly fed, hydrated, bathed, and groomed,' Mom says. 'Frankly, she wasn't placed a day too soon. We've never seen her so confused.'

'Gee, wonder why? You barge into her home, practically

give her a stroke, and she ends up in emergency. Then you move her stuff around, and when she defends herself from a break-in, she gets locked up in a strange place getting orders from people she doesn't know. And she's confused? No kidding.'

'Honey, it's hard what's happening to Granny,' Dad says, 'but you can't keep making excuses.'

'I'm not making excuses. I'm pointing out facts. Plus another fact: they've stuffed her with drugs, haven't they?'

Dad squirms. 'She's only on anti-depressants and sedatives. They're to make her happy.'

'Well, guess what: she isn't. So here's an idea. Give *me* her meds. That way she'll get her brain back, and I can forget you exist.' I turn up the volume and bang down the hall to my room.

Why do they have to be them? Why do I have to be me?

I get a couple of calls in the middle of the night. It must be too dark for Granny to read her hand. I turn off the ring and change my message: 'If this is Granny, you're not at home, but everything's okay. Detective Bird will see you in the morning. Till then: Rhubarb!'

When I wake up Sunday morning I have seven messages:

'Pie! Okay then.'

'Pie! I can't wait till morning.'

'Pie! Where's Teddy?'

'Pie! Is that the cemetery out there?'

'Pie! Is this a dream?'

'Pie! Bring Teddy.'

'Pie! It's morning. Where are you?'

Naturally, we can't go to Greenview right away 'cause that would be too easy. Instead we have to go to church first. Why? 'Cause 'We never miss church, you know that.'

'Yeah,' I roll my eyes. 'God's all, "People are starving, but stop the world — the Birds aren't at church."'

'Watch your mouth.'

I sit in the pew like a zombie with brushed teeth. Pastor Nolan goes on about joy everlasting, but the only thing everlasting is his sermon. Afterwards, we go to Swiss Chalet.

'Why don't we bring Granny?'

You'd think I screamed: Release the Kraken! 'One day,' Mom says. 'First, Granny needs to get used to where she is.'

Dad nods. 'If we bring her out now, we'll need a Taser to get her back.'

I wolf down my food and skip dessert to get to Greenview faster. What does Mom do? Slows down. Apparently 'learning to enjoy your food,' means chewing till your jaw falls off.

'Wasn't that lovely,' she says, patting her lips with a serviette.

'You've got coleslaw in your teeth.'

We finally pull into Greenview.

'Behave or else,' Mom says.

My head is full of swears I didn't know I knew.

'Granny's room is the second window from the left on the third floor,' Dad says. 'She has a perfect view of Grampa's grave. When she's thinking of Grampa she can just look outside and there he is. Isn't that nice?'

Are you for real?

We sign in at the reception desk, which is between a tuck shop and a sliding door to a small courtyard garden. They've put me on the official visitors' list as a peace offering. The woman behind the desk is a perky cheerleader from sometime last century. I've never seen her in town, which is probably why she smiles at me. 'So you're Zoe. I'm Amy. You're all your grandmother talks about.'

Okay, so she's a *nice* perky cheerleader. 'Granny's all I think about, too.'

We go up the elevator and through the security door into Granny's ward. There's a nurses' desk at the end of a big recreation room: a few couches and dining-room tables on the right; on the left, a semi-circle of people in wheelchairs staring at a TV with their mouths open.

'Isn't this a nice place?' Mom says, as we walk to the corridor beyond the nurses' station. 'It doesn't smell of pee.'

'Let's check for that on Trip Advisor. "Great hotel. It doesn't smell of pee."'

Before Mom can say anything, the nurse from behind the desk introduces herself – 'Hi, I'm Lisa' – and we go down the corridor to Granny's room.

'The room is small,' Dad says, 'but it's private and it has its own bathroom. The food's better than she's been getting, too. Also, they give her two baths a week and her clothes are name-tagged so nothing will go missing in the wash.'

'Don't forget the entertainment, Tim,' Mom adds. 'Sing-a longs. Bingo. It's like summer camp for seniors. Granny won't be all alone in a house full of moulds. And think of the company.'

'Yeah. Like Dr Rutherford. Granny hates him. He's a perv.'

'Zoe,' Dad pleads.

Outside each door there's a glass case with pictures, medals and figurines. Dad says they're to remind people which room is theirs. Through the doorways, I see old people staring out their windows. I bet they're waiting for visitors who never come. Granny won't be like that. I'll be here every day.

We get to Granny's. Her memory box has a picture of her and Grampa and us. *How about a bird nest?*

Dad knocks. 'Mother. Guess who's come to visit.'

'About time.' Granny's sitting on her bed in a plain top, black sweat pants and her black sweater, her red leather purse slung over her shoulder. The closets and dresser drawers are open and empty. Her clothes are in a sack she's made with a bedsheet. Her paintings are propped against the garden gnome.

'Mother . . .'

Granny stands up. 'I'm all packed. Take me home.'

'You *are* home, Grace,' Mom says.

'I was talking to my son.'

'Carrie's right, Mother,' Dad says. 'This is your home now.'

'This is *not* my home. My home is the Bird House, 125 Maple Street. Your father died in that house and your grandfather and your great-grandfather. It's where *I'm* going to die, too. There are my things. Make yourself useful.'

I pick up the sack of clothes.

'Put that down,' Dad says. 'Don't make this difficult, Mother.'

'Difficult for whom?'

'For all of us.'

'I won't stay, Tim. There's people yelling nonsense. If you're not crazy when you come here, you soon will be.' Granny holds onto Dad. 'Please. Whatever I've done, forgive me. Just don't leave me here.'

'I'll be waiting in the car,' Mom says quietly. She leaves, a hand brushing her eyes.

'I'm sorry, Mother. We'll come back when you're rested.' Dad gently removes her hands from his arms. She sinks onto the bed. He gives me a glance. 'Say goodbye, Zoe.'

'Dad, let me stay. I'll get Granny settled.'

He shifts from one foot to the other; you can practically hear the sweat squish between his toes. 'Fine. But be home by dinner.'

13

Granny and I sit by the window and watch Mom and Dad drive away. Her chairs and mattress belong to Greenview. Apparently they worry about bringing in bedbugs in people's furniture – which, hello, Granny's doesn't have.

'I need Teddy.' She fiddles with her wedding ring. 'If Teddy knew what was happening . . .'

'Uncle Teddy's gone, Granny.'

'Gone, gone. Why did it have to be like that?'

'Granny, whatever it was, it's not your fault.'

'Teddy. I need him. He wouldn't leave me like this. Not if he knew.'

'I saw a courtyard on my way in,' I go. 'Would you like to go there?'

'What?'

'There are flowers. Would you like to see some flowers?'

'Flowers?' She looks confused. 'Are there daffodils?'

'Let's see.'

We walk down the corridor arm in arm. 'We're going to the courtyard,' I tell Nurse Lisa.

'Have fun.' She nods me over. 'To unlock the exit, tap in the code that's over the keypad by the door.'

'Why have a code if everyone can see it?'

'To keep the residents from wandering.'

'You mean they can't figure it out?'

'Not on this floor.'

I glance at Granny, peering around the room in bewilderment. *Will Mom and Dad ever get like that? Will I?*

I punch in the code, the door opens, and I take Granny down the elevator. She's not upset any more. *What's she thinking? Does she know where we are?*

Amy gives us a wave from the reception desk: 'Mrs Bird, how nice to see you.'

'How nice to see *you*,' Granny nods vaguely.

'Enjoy yourselves.' Amy presses a button behind her desk; the doors to the courtyard slide open. We walk into the garden, sit on a bench and check out the flowers. Granny pats her thighs and frowns. She looks down at her sweat pants. 'Where's my dress?'

That's what I've been wondering. 'At the dry cleaners.'

'Remind me to pick it up.'

For the next couple of hours, she rests her head on my shoulder and I stroke her hair.

'I feel fuzzy,' she says. 'My head's moss. I think I should have a lie-down.'

'Whatever you say.' I bring us back to the elevator.

'Where are we going?' Granny asks.

'Upstairs.'

'Why?'

'So you can nap.'

'I think I'd be better off on the comfy couch.'

All the same, she takes my arm, gets in the elevator with me, and lets me lead her down the hall to her room. She stops dead when she sees the photos in her memory box.

'What are those doing here?'

'Mom and Dad thought you'd like them.'

'They belong at home.'

'We'll get them there.' I walk us into her room. The support workers have put everything back the way Mom and Dad had it.

'I dreamt I was in this room.' Granny's forehead twitches; she opens the closet. 'What are my clothes doing here? I can *see* me taking them out.' She turns to the night table, runs over, and moves the family pictures around. 'Where's Teddy? He's gone.'

'It's okay, Granny. I'll get you his picture by tomorrow.'

'Good. I need Teddy. I can't forget Teddy.'

'You won't ever forget Uncle Teddy.' I sit beside her on the bed. 'It must've been awful when he died.'

Granny gasps. 'Teddy died?'

I squeeze her hand. 'Yes, Granny. Years ago, in Elmira.'

'Teddy never died in Elmira. He moved to Toronto.' Granny says. 'I have cards and letters. He has a new place. There's a park across the street.'

'Granny, are you maybe confused?'

'No. Are you?'

A support worker pops in and out of the room. 'Dinner time, Mrs Bird.'

'I'm with my granddaughter,' she calls after him.

'Actually, I should be going.' I get up.

'I'll go with you.'

'Granny, I'm afraid you can't come.'

'Why not?'

'Mom and Dad. If I bring you home, they'll bring you back and never let me see you on my own again. Understand?' Her eyes say no. 'Don't worry. You won't be here long. I'll get you back to the Bird House soon.'

'All right then. I'm counting on you.' Granny hugs me. 'I can always count on you, can't I?'

'You bet.'

I get to the elevator as fast as I can. When I step outside to the parking lot, Granny's at her window, waving down at me: *She remembered I was visiting. If she was at the Bird House . . . If she wasn't on those drugs . . . If it weren't for Mom and Dad . . .*

I walk backwards. We blow each other kisses. Finally, the trees block our view, and I can run away without her seeing me cry.

When I get home, our Carrie's House of Hair sign is blinking up the front window. I'm too mad to be embarrassed. Mom and Dad are sipping lemonade on the verandah. I storm up the driveway.

'Back on time. Good,' Dad says, like we're off to a new start.

'Nice visit?' from Mom.

'Whose idea was it to put Granny in sweat pants?'

'Shh!' Mom looks at the hedge, afraid the neighbours are listening. 'Elastic waistbands are easier for staff when Granny goes to the bathroom.'

'She goes to the bathroom on her own.'

'Not on time.'

'What about you in Mexico? Plus another thing. Where's Uncle Teddy's picture? You thought Granny wouldn't notice? She does.'

'What are you talking about?' Dad goes. 'If it got mislaid, I'll find it.'

'First, why don't you find Uncle Teddy. He's "mislaid" in Toronto, right?'

Dad's lemonade spurts through his nose. Mom makes that sound with her straw.

'You let me think he died in Elmira. He's not even dead, is he?'

Their eyes dart back and forth like rabbits.

'Might as well be.' Dad's face is ashes.

'What do you mean, "might as well be"?'

'Teddy took off when I was seven,' Dad says.

'Why?'

'None of your business.'

'Says who?'

71

'Says I'm your father.'

Says what are you hiding? 'Granny wants to see him.'

'Well, Teddy doesn't want to see her.'

'I don't believe you.'

'Was Teddy at your grampa's funeral? No! Not at your great-grandpa's, either. No matter what your granny wants, it's too late.'

'If you're so sure, call him. Have him say it.'

Dad squeezes his plastic cup so hard it cracks. Blood runs down his hand. 'Now see what you've done!' He runs into the house, Mom after him: 'Tim, wait. Let me get you a tea towel.'

So Granny isn't crazy: Uncle Teddy *is* alive. And in Toronto. I grab my phone and search for his number on Canada 411. There are dozens of Birds in the city, but no T for Ted or E for Edward. *Oh no. Maybe he has a cell.* I check Facebook, Twitter, a bunch of sites. No luck.

I slump on the verandah steps. *Granny says she's had cards and letters, but what if they're old? What if he's moved again? Or won't help? What if her hopes are a dream?*

But what if they're not?

14

Monday morning, I arrive at school as the buses come in from the country. Suckhole's waiting for Dylan. We pretend not to see each other. I lock my bike and start to head inside.

'Zoe, wait up,' Ricky calls out. He lopes over from his bus. 'About your grandmother. Just so you know, the same thing's happening to my gramps. It's hard.' He shuffles. 'I'm thinking about you.'

Did I just hear that? 'Thank you.'

He blushes, 'You're welcome. It was nothing. Just, you know.' He leans in, totally serious. 'I told Madi she should apologise for what she said about your grandmother.'

'She won't.'

'She should.'

My heart fills. 'Whatever. It means a lot you told her off.'

Ricky goes to say something else, but stops. He gives me this shy, lopsided grin and disappears.

I'm a puddle of happy. Especially 'cause Suckhole's jaw is on the asphalt. I go to geography in a bliss bubble: *Ricky cares about me. Ohmigod. When he leaned in – gosh he smells great. What did he want to say when he left?*

Stop it. Don't get your hopes up.

Why not? He told Suckhole to apologise! He wouldn't do that if I didn't matter.

All morning, I go from thinking about Ricky, to drawing pictures of Mom and Dad in Hell. Mom's wig is stuffed in her mouth to stop the screaming. Satan's shoved his pitchfork up Dad's ass.

At lunch, I shoot Ricky a smile. He smiles back. I melt 'cause the *way* he does it is, well, so sweet I almost go up and sit with him, only I'm too scared to wreck it. For the first time in ages, I eat without wanting to heave.

That is, until right before the bell. Suckhole and the Suckhole-ettes plunk themselves down at my table without even asking.

'Poor you,' Suckhole goes. 'I'd be *so* upset if my grand-mother attacked a guy with a butcher's knife. Good thing she's locked up, hunh?'

I throw my Coke in her face and march out of the caf staring straight ahead.

'Zoe, it's okay,' she calls, running after me. 'I forgive you. I know how hard this must be.' A crowd follows us, hungry for action.

Don't run. Don't cry. It's what she wants.

'Hold up. It's just that I love you so much,' she pleads. 'I want your granny to get the help she needs.'

If I can make it to the bathroom, lock myself in a stall, stick my fingers in my ears—

Suckhole grabs me by my elbow. 'Please, Zoe, I care.'

I whirl round. 'Bullshit. You're a stupid suckhole, that's what you are. And your dad's a drunk. His uncle passed out on the train tracks. Dogs ate his guts.'

'That's a lie!'

'Says who, you stupid ho?' I tap her on the shoulder.

Suckhole throws herself back against the lockers like I'm She-Hulk. She drops to the floor screaming, 'Help! Make her stop!'

Everybody's, 'Fight! Fight!'

Dylan grabs me from behind. I flail away, kick his shins: 'Let go of me!' *Is Ricky here? Is he seeing this? Please no.*

Mr Jeffries wades through the crowd, underarm stains on his shirt, his breath like scrambled eggs. 'Freeze!' He kneels down, puts his arm round Suckhole. 'Are you all right?'

'I don't know,' she sobs.

'It's Zoe's fault,' Caitlyn squeals. 'She beat on her for nothing.'

Mr Jeffries glares at me. He takes us to Vice-Principal Watson, Suckhole limping on his arm.

Mr Watson frowns. 'What happened?'

'She started it,' I say.

He shushes me and looks to Princess Suckhole.

'Zoe called me a h-h-ho and slammed me against the lockers and I was just saying I wished her granny well after what happened at the Bird House.'

Mr Watson suspends me for three days.

* * *

Back home, my parents sit me down at the kitchen table.

Mom pulls out a hankie: 'How will we face your Aunt Jess and Uncle Chad?'

On your hands and knees, like always?

Dad slams his hand on the table. 'You're grounded for a month. And we're taking your phone.'

'Not again!'

'*Two* months,' Dad says. 'Madi tried to be nice and what did you do? Threw Coke in her face, tore into her family, tossed her to the ground—'

'That's not how it happened.'

'Your granny, she works you up. No more Granny till the weekend.'

'I hate you. I wish you were dead.'

Mom's lip trembles. 'What did we do to deserve this?'

'You got pregnant, that's what. Why didn't you get rid of me? I wish you had.' I run to my room, smother my face in my pillow. A whirlwind of hollers. 'LEAVE ME ALONE LEAVE ME ALONE LEAVE ME ALONE!!!' I keep it up till they do.

15

Tuesday noon. We've been summoned to Aunt Jess and Uncle Chad's for lunch, so I'm in my church clothes. I feel like a reject from *Convent Runway*. We park on the street 'cause Uncle Chad's moved their mini-vans from the garage to the driveway.

'Did you bring the umbrella?' I ask as we dodge their sprinkler.

'Behave.'

Dad does his shave-and-a-haircut tap with the lion's head knocker. Naturally, they make us wait. Dad raps two more times. Finally, Aunt Jess opens the door. 'Come in,' she says, like this is a pleasant surprise.

'Shall we take off our shoes?' Dad asks hopefully.

'No, leave them on.'

Wise.

Uncle Chad's wearing an open-neck polo shirt: his chest hair looks like a Brillo pad. 'Have a seat.' He points us to their leatherette sectional.

'I'd forgotten how lovely your place is,' Mom says, looking around at all the gold frames and zebra rugs.

'Well, it's home.' Aunt Jess wheels in her mother's

antique trolley with coffee, cucumber sandwiches and Sarah Lee brownies. Everybody gets served except me. Aunt Jess and Uncle Chad lean back in their matching La-Z-Boys.

'It hasn't been a happy week, has it?' Aunt Jess sighs.

Mom shakes her head. 'It surely hasn't. Please know we're sorry about the incident at the school yesterday. Aren't we, Zoe?'

I suck it up and nod.

Aunt Jess looks to Uncle Chad. He folds his hands across his belly. 'So, Tim . . . How do you propose we handle the situation?'

'No need for you and Jess to fuss yourselves.' Dad shifts in his seat. 'Carrie and I can take care of things.'

'Oh?'

'Not that it's your fault,' Aunt Jess interrupts. 'We haven't had to deal with a challenge like yours, have we, Chad?'

Hello, I'm in the room.

Uncle Chad keeps staring at Dad.

Say something, Dad. He's making you look stupid!

'If you weren't family, there'd be lawsuits.' Uncle Chad says. 'Assault's a serious matter.'

'Assault.' Dad heh-hehs. 'That's a little extreme, isn't it?'

'Not after the threats.'

'What threats?' Mom goes whiter than china.

'Madi's friends, Katie and Caitlyn, have told us things we can't repeat,' Aunt Jess says.

'Whatever they said, they're lying,' I go.

Everyone stares at me like I'm a bug on Planet Squish Me.

Aunt Jess bites her lip. 'There's also the slanders against our family. Zoe told everyone that Chad's uncle passed out on the train tracks. She said dogs ate his . . . I can't even say it.'

Mom covers her mouth.

'Of course, our main concern is the young woman upstairs crying her eyes out,' Uncle Chad says. 'What hurts her the most is, she was attacked by her cousin; the best friend she's defended all these years.'

What?

Dad looks at me sternly, so Uncle Chad will think he's tough. 'What do you have to say?'

How about, Bite me? 'Sorry.'

'Perhaps you'd like to tell Madi that?' Aunt Jess calls up the stairs. 'Honey, your cousin has something to say to you.'

Suckhole limps down the stairs on the opposite foot from yesterday. Aunt Jess gives up her La-Z-Boy, and plumps herself on the armrest, holding Suckhole's hand.

I look at the centre of Suckhole's forehead. 'I'm sorry about yesterday.'

Saint Suckhole bats her eyes. 'I forgive you. I'm really sad about your granny. I'm sorry if you heard me wrong.'

Uncle Chad tosses my folks a look that says, *That's-how-to-raise-a-daughter.*

'Zoe,' Mom nudges me, 'would you like to say, "Thank you, Madi"?'

'Thank you, Madi. I'm sorry if I heard you wrong, too. Your parents said I was your best friend. That's why I didn't understand when you said I couldn't sit with you in the caf, or talk to you, or be treated like a human being.'

'Pardon?' Apparently Aunt Jess has a hearing problem.

I bat my eyes. 'Madi says I can't even say hello, I'm such a loser.'

The grown-ups look shocked, 'cause, of course, Saint Suckhole would never say such a thing.

Suckhole takes a deep breath and goes for the Oscar. 'I'm so sorry I said that. I was just worried about my reputation. I was afraid people might think I do what *you* do because we're cousins.'

'Like what?' I go.

'Don't make me say.'

'Madi, if there's something your aunt and uncle should hear, you need to tell them,' Uncle Chad says.

'It may not even be true,' Suckhole says. 'You know how boys talk.'

I leap up. 'That is so—'

'Sit!' Dad orders.

'But—'

'Sit!!!'

I do. Why? 'Cause everyone's staring at me that's why. 'Cause it doesn't matter what I say, that's why. 'Cause I'm me and she's her, that's why.

'You go upstairs and rest,' Aunt Jess tells Suckhole.

Poor Herself wobbles to her feet with an *ow* face. 'It was nice seeing you, Aunt Carrie, Uncle Tim. When you're back at school, Zoe, please sit at my table again.' With that, Our Lady of Perpetual Bullshit hops up the stairs on one foot.

Uncle Chad and Aunt Jess stare at my parents. Mom and Dad look like they want to hide under the tea trolley.

'You'll recall that boarding school Chad told you about last summer?' Aunt Jess passes Mom a brochure from the trolley. 'It's tough love, dawn to dusk.'

'YOU GUYS WANT TO SHIP ME TO BOARD-ING SCHOOL?'

She looks at me like I've made her point. I shrink.

'I guess that's it then,' Uncle Chad says. He and Aunt Jess show us out. They pretend not to notice we're soaked by the sprinkler.

Mom rocks in her car seat as we turn the corner. 'I've never been so embarrassed.'

'At least not *today*,' I mutter.

Dad grips the wheel. 'This isn't a joke. One more problem and you *will* be off to that school, even if it takes the store money.'

'You'd lock me up like Granny?'

'We can't let you ruin your life,' Dad says. 'We love you.'

I cross my arms and stare out the window. 'Right.' *See if I ever tell you anything again.*

16

As soon as we get back, I go to the kitchen landline and call Granny.

'Granny, hi. If you've been calling, sorry, I haven't got your messages. Mom and Dad took my phone. They say I can't see you till the weekend.'

'What?' Granny says. 'Put your dad on.'

I hold out the receiver. 'Granny wants to talk to you.' Dad glares at me. 'Well, she does.'

He takes the phone. 'Mother, Zoe didn't give you the full picture. She had an incident with Madi.'

'Madi?' Granny's so angry I can hear her across the kitchen. 'What did that little brat do to Zoe this time?'

'It wasn't Madi's fault, Mother . . . Mother, calm down . . . Please, Mother . . .'

I give Mom and Dad a finger wave and disappear into my room. If I was Uncle Teddy, I'd take off. Mom and Dad wouldn't miss me. They'd be glad I wasn't around to embarrass them. I almost wish I was dead, only then Suckhole would make it all about her. She'd be Mourner-In-Chief, guys lined up with Kleenex boxes.

Mom knocks on my door. 'Dinner.'

'I'm not hungry.'

'Suit yourself.'

I come out two hours later. Mom and Dad are sitting in the dryer chairs watching a stupid TV show. My meal is on the table. Cold lasagne and Jello.

'We've decided it's best if your Granny doesn't have her cell phone any more. It gets her upset.'

I pretend I don't hear. I pretend I don't care. They are *so* going to pay.

Next morning at breakfast, I don't say anything; just grin like a puppet.

'Sleep well?'

Nod.

'What are you thinking?'

Shrug.

'Say something.'

Eyebrows up: *What?*

Back in my room I get ready for round two.

Mom's gals start arriving at nine o'clock. Today is special 'cause a lot of them haven't seen her since Granny's lock-up. They're all, 'Carrie, you're a saint.' I wait till the place is jammed, then make my entrance.

Mom's washing Mrs Connelly's hair; Mrs Stuart is under a dryer; the rest are at the dinette set. When they see me, they freeze.

'Good morning,' I say with a big smile.

They look surprised, 'cause all I've ever done before is grunt. I pick up a hairdo magazine, and sit in a roller chair.

'So, Zoe,' Mrs Connelly says, 'is school off today?'

'For me,' I say, sweeter than Suckhole. 'I got suspended for tapping my cousin Madi. Apparently she's dying.'

'That's not funny,' Mom says.

'Sorry,' I go like a scolded puppy. 'I'm actually very concerned.'

Mom gives me That Look.

'Well, I am. Seriously. I'm whatever you want me to be.' *Go ahead. Yell at me and look like a crazy person.*

Mom's beyond tense: I imagine her drowning Mrs Connelly in the sink by accident. I mime zipping my lips with a finger and go back to reading. The gals squirm and stare at the TV where some morning show guest is going on about chasing tornados in a jeep.

After the gals leave, Mom's so mad I expect her wig to melt. 'Don't ever do that again.'

'What?'

'You know what.'

I check my nails. 'You've always told me to socialise.'

At dinner, Mom tells Dad about me making a spectacle of myself. *Yeah, I'm a one-girl Cirque du Soleil.* They lecture me about a bunch of stuff. Consideration? Respect? Growing up? I'm not really sure 'cause I'm not really listening: I'm staring at Mom's wig. She fusses with it. Dad sweats up a storm. Cool.

'Blah blah blah!' Dad throws down his napkin.

'Blah blah blah!' Mom pushes back her chair.

'Thanks for the meal,' I go. 'We must do this again sometime.'

Thursday I spend the day missing Granny. When I'm bored I go to the bathroom. 'Don't worry, I'm not coming out,' I holler for the gals. 'I just have to pee!' I also make up satanic spells and try them on Suckhole. Apparently they don't work any better than prayers. If they did, there'd have been a big *Ka-boom* from the high school.

At dinner we're like robots studying Conversational Human. Mom daubs her eyes with her serviette. Dad's eyebrows do push-ups. Back in my room, I flop on the bed and stare at the ceiling fan.

What would happen if I stuck my head between the fan blades?

I hear Mom talking to Dad. 'Greenview called this afternoon. They can't get your mother to bathe. They've tried the last three mornings. She throws things at them.'

If you woke with strangers trying to take off your clothes, wouldn't you?

I go to the bathroom, fill up the tub, stick my head underwater and scream.

17

Friday morning. First period back in school, I slump in my seat, jacket on, daring Ms Bundy to ask me a question. She doesn't. Good.

Suckhole shows up for English, period two. She's got crutches plastered with autographs and happy-face stickers. She glances back at me from the front. *DIE, BITCH, DIE.* At the bell, she waits by the door like she wants to talk. I push past like she isn't there. She catches up with me at my locker.

'Stalker much?' I dump my books.

'Zoe . . .'

'What?'

She bites her lip. 'I've been thinking—'

'That's a first.'

'Please, Zoe. You're right. I've been a total bitch.'

'Tell me about it. No, don't. I'm having lunch.' I grab my sandwich bag and head outside across the parking lot.

Suckhole speed-hops after me. 'I never meant for things to get so weird. That awful stuff – I don't know how it happened.'

'It happened because you did it.'

'So fine, be like that. Blame me for everything. You're perfect and I'm horrible and I got you in trouble. But I want to make things right.'

'Like Hell. What do you really want?'

Suckhole goes sobby. 'Only to invite you to a party Saturday night.'

'Nice try. There isn't even going to be a party, is there? You want to get me all excited and when I show up to wherever, there won't be anybody there and you'll laugh at me like you always do.'

'I won't!' Suckhole pulls out a Kleenex. 'Dylan's throwing a surprise party for Ricky making the football team. There'll just be a couple of guys plus me, Katie and Caitlyn. The guys are bringing him out at eleven o'clock after the late show. Come with me.'

'What's the deal?'

'There's no deal.'

'There is too. No way you want to bring me to a party.'

'Okay, you're right, I *don't*.' She stuffs the Kleenex back in her pocket. 'But apparently Ricky likes you, don't ask me why. He's told me a million times to apologise for the granny stuff. I'm like, seriously? Only he's Dylan's friend. If you're there 'cause of me, he'll be off my case. But stay home, fine, I'll live. In fact, forget I asked.' She tosses her hair and hops back across the asphalt.

My feet twist like crazy. *So Ricky* did *tell her to apologise.*

What he said, it's true. 'Madi! Wait!' I catch up. 'Okay, fine, I'll come.'

'Too late. You had your chance.'

'I'm sorry. I wasn't thinking.'

She keeps hopping like she can't hear me.

I open the door for her. 'I mean it. Bring me to the party and I'll tell Ricky you apologised. I'll even say you meant it.'

'Shh!' She stops, real cross as people pass us. 'It's a surprise! You want the world to know?'

'Sorry, sorry.'

'That's what you always say. But fine.'

'Thanks. There's just one little problem. How do I get to Dylan's farm?'

'You mean we have to drive you?' she asks like I'm three.

'Please? I can sneak out after Mom and Dad are in bed.'

'When's that?'

'Ten.'

'That's cutting it close.'

'I know, but I'm grounded except for school, remember?'

'Fine.' She rolls her eyes like it's totally not. 'Dylan and I will be in his Dad's SUV at the park down from your place at ten fifteen. We have to be back to Dylan's before Ricky, so if you're late, we leave without you. And not another word or you're uninvited.'

I nod *Okay*.

For the rest of the day, I float around the halls. I bump into Ricky after the final bell.

'Good to see you back.' He shoots me his special grin. 'How was your suspension?'

'Fine.' I blush. 'Guess you saw my so-called fight?'

He shakes his head. 'I'd gone outside to study for a history test.'

'Good. It was kind of embarrassing.'

'She deserved it. Anyway, have to get my bus.' He waves. 'See you later.'

'Yeah.' *Tonight at your party, ha ha.* I picture us finding ourselves in a private corner accidentally on purpose. I picture us hugging. I picture – *Breathe. Breathe.*

18

Saturday morning, I pull a shopping bag down from the back of my top shelf. Inside is a skirt and halter top I bought with last year's Christmas money. Mom said no way I could wear them – 'The skirt's too high and the top's too low' – but I refused to take them back and they've been there ever since.

I've grown a bit, so the skirt's even shorter and the top's tighter. Perfect. *Unless my parents catch me wearing them.* They won't. *But if?* Okay, they'll kill me, but I'll already be dead for sneaking out so who cares?

I also think about make-up. I want to wear some for Ricky, only I'm scared to do it wrong. There's a starter kit in the bottom of my underwear drawer that Mom got for me after Aunt Jess got one for Suckhole. First day I had it, I ran to Suckhole for tips. She looked at me like, *Don't you know anything?* Mom tried to help, only she was such a backseat driver I ended up looking like the Joker.

From then on, I made a big deal about not wanting to look fake. 'How about not looking ugly?' Suckhole said. Ha ha, only now I wish I'd listened. I wish I'd practised. I go to YouTube and click on *Applying Mascara like a Pro* and *Do-It-Yourself Beauty Tips*. Maybe it's not so hard after all.

Mid-afternoon I take time for a quick visit with Granny, our first all week thanks to Mom and Dad. Her paintings are beside her night table next to the garden gnome and her bedsheet-sack. She's on her hands and knees looking under the bed.

'Rhubarb pie, Granny.'

She pops her head up. 'Pumpkin!'

'What are you looking for?'

Granny shrugs. 'Whatever it was wasn't there. But come. Sit.' She pats a place beside her on the bed. 'I've made a decision. I'm seeing your uncle Teddy in Toronto. Come with me.'

'Uh, Granny, I don't think this is a good day for travelling.'

'Why not?'

'Because.'

'Because why?'

'Because Mom and Dad. Also how would we get there? The train's in Woodstock and I can't drive.'

'I can, silly.'

'You haven't been on the highway for years.'

'So what?' Granny says. 'I could get us to Woodstock.'

'We'd need trip money. Tickets, food.'

'I have a money stash at home.'

'Where?'

'The less you know.' Granny taps her nose. 'Come. Please. I need you. I forget what's what sometimes. But if you were with me, you'd know what to do till I was right again.'

Okay. Truth time. I take her hand. 'Granny, this is hard to say, but what if we went to Toronto and Uncle Teddy didn't want to see you?'

'He would.'

'He wasn't at Grampa's funeral.'

Granny's eyes flicker. 'They didn't get along.'

'It's more than that. Uncle Teddy hasn't come home for anything. You say he writes, but Dad puts your mail in the front hall. I haven't seen his name on anything.'

'Don't confuse me.' She squeezes my hand. 'No matter what happened, Teddy won't let me die here.'

'Granny, we don't even know if he's still in Toronto.'

'He has to be.'

'His number's not listed. He could've moved.'

'No!' She presses her face into my shoulder. 'I need to see him again. Just once. I need to tell him I'm sorry. I need him to forgive me.'

'For what?'

'Everything.'

There's a terrible silence. I let her hang in my arms, then pull away. 'I have to get ready for something, Granny. But I'll be back tomorrow. We can talk about it then. Okay?'

Granny doesn't say anything. I back out of her room. Outside in the parking lot, I look up to her room. She's not at her window.

19

When Mom and Dad took my phone last summer, they got me a watch so I wouldn't have an excuse for being late. Correction, they got me a pink plastic piece of crap with the *Frozen* princesses on it. Right now it's ten minutes past Princess Anna's right eyeball and dinner is finally over.

Tuna casserole. Did I really need fish breath?

I brush my teeth for like half an hour, then I go to my room, get into my party clothes, and throw a dressing gown over top in case my parents come in. Also for parents, I wait to put on my make-up. To pass time, I stare in the mirror and practise my smile.

Topics of conversation. What do we have in common? Grandparents losing it. How romantic. *I know, we'll talk about him making the team, his friends, his smile.*

I want to bite my nails to the knuckle. I sit on my hands.

Okay, it's eight thirty. I open my starter kit. Here goes nothing. I work out the cracks around the rims of my blush pots and moisten my mascara with a little rubbing alcohol. Hope I don't get an eye infection.

Eight fifty. I like the lashes and liner. Now for the lipstick and blush.

Nine o'clock. Not bad. I should add a few sparkles for luck . . . I need a few more . . . So maybe I didn't.

Five past nine. I remove some sparkles, but mess up the highlighter. I smooth things out with a finger . . . Grr, the left side has less colour than the right . . . Now the right side has less colour than the left . . . Okay, I should leave it. If the lights are too bright, I can wash it off before Ricky gets there.

Nine thirty. Mom and Dad are still watching Mom's favourite reality show in the salon. I brush my hair to keep calm.

Nine forty-five. Why does time take fffooorrreeev-vveeerrr.

Ten o'clock. The TV goes off. 'I can't believe they sent the redhead home. Can you believe it, Tim? Tim? Tim, are you asleep?'

'What?'

'You always fall asleep on me.'

'Sorry. The Pams kicked in too quick.'

'You watch those pills. It's every night now,' Mom says on their way to the bathroom. They brush their teeth. *Hurry up.* They close the door to their room.

Ten past ten. *Suckhole, don't leave!*

I tiptoe down the hall and out the side door. Dylan's SUV is idling at the park. I race the whole way, waving my arms for them to see me in the rear-view mirror.

Suckhole and Dylan are in the front seats. Katie and Caitlyn are in the back.

'We have dibs on the window seats,' Caitlyn says and gets out to let me in. I sit between them.

'You got away okay?' Suckhole asks as we head out of town.

'Yeah. It took Mom and Dad for ever to go to bed. Sorry I kept you waiting.'

'No problem.' She hands me a rum cooler.

I hate drinking, but I don't want to look stupid so I take it. 'Thanks.'

Katie and Caitlyn giggle. *Are they drunk already?*

There's only a couple of other cars on the road. The farms are dark. I take a sip from my cooler. Dylan's place is coming up on the right. We drive past it.

'Isn't the party at Dylan's?'

'Change of plans.'

'So where is it?'

'You'll see.'

I look from Katie to Caitlyn. They're grinning.

I try to stay calm. 'There *is* a party, right?'

'Sure,' Suckhole says. 'Just not the one you were expecting.'

'Okay.' My voice quivers. 'But Ricky, he'll be there?'

'Afraid he can't make it. Real shame, hunh, with you dressed up so nice? Not that he'd care. See, he doesn't actually like you. He feels sorry for you.'

'Let me out.'

'I don't think so. Katie. Caitlyn.'

They press tight against me. *My phone. How could my folks take my phone?* The drink can crumples in my hand. Rum cooler spills all over me.

'Aw, you've wet your Band-Aid; I mean your skirt,' Katie snickers. 'What's underneath? Special Ricky panties?' They laugh. *Breathe. Breathe.*

We turn onto the old McClennan Sideroad, an abandoned dirt lane, and drive to a rusty bridge. Dylan cuts the engine and kills the headlights. Everything's swallowed in night.

Suckhole shines a flashlight in my face; Katie starts recording on her phone. 'Get out.'

'What are you going to do?'

'Guess.'

The doors open. Suckhole and Dylan get out. I lunge forward to press the horn. Caitlyn grabs my waist and yanks me back. I try to cling to Suckhole's headrest. It slips through my fingers. I fall outside onto the gravel.

Suckhole nods to Dylan. 'Do like I told you.'

He grabs me under the arms and hauls me to the middle of the bridge.

I struggle. 'Help!'

'Like anyone's going to hear you.'

Caitlyn kicks dirt at me. 'You so deserve this.'

'Totally,' Katie says, half-falling down from doing her video. Dylan sits me on the railing. Suckhole shines her flashlight off the bridge. Down below is a creek bed: rocks, broken glass, and strings of barbed-wire.

'Please don't hurt me.'

'We'll do what we want.' Suckhole's eyes tighten. 'What makes you think you can disrespect me? Shove me down in front of everyone? Make me look bad in front of my folks?'

'I'm sorry. I'm sorry.'

'You're a sorry piece of shit is what you are. Well, it's payback time.'

'What kind of payback?'

'I want to hear you say, "Spit on me. I'm a Bird Turd."'

'What?'

'You heard me. Say, "Spit on me. I'm a Bird Turd."'

'No.'

Suckhole gives Dylan a signal. He raises his hands like he's going to push me.

'No! Don't! I'll die!'

'So?'

'If I don't come home there'll be questions.'

'Not for us. We aren't even here. We're at my place studying. My parents will back me up. You know it, too.'

'Anyway,' Katie says, recording, 'everyone'll think you ran away.'

'And when they find me?'

'Guess you killed yourself.'

'So say it,' Suckhole goes. '"Spit on me. I'm a Bird Turd." Say it or else.'

I glance down at the rocks, start shaking like crazy. 'Okay, okay. Spit on me. I'm a Bird Turd.'

Suckhole grins and horks in my face. They all do. 'Now say: "Granny's a dirty bird. She's Granny Bird Turd."'

'Madi, no. I can't. Anything about me, but not about Granny.'

'Say it now.' Suckhole punches the flashlight hard into my chest. It knocks me backwards. My calves grip the railing – they start to slip – I flail with my arms – I'm going to fall. 'AAA!'

Dylan grabs my legs at the knees. I hang upside down screaming.

Katie laughs. 'Hey, think Bird Turd can fly?'

'Pull me up!'

'Why?' Caitlyn taunts.

'Last chance,' Suckhole goes. '"Granny's a dirty bird. She's Granny Bird Turd!"'

'Dylan! Please! Pull me up and I'll tell you about her cousin Danny. You know, from Saskatoon?'

'SHUT YOUR FACE!' Suckhole yells at me.

Dylan twists sideways to Suckhole. 'What's this about Danny?'

She grabs at his arms. 'Don't listen to the little bitch. Drop her.'

'No! Dylan! Pull me up! I'll tell you everything!'

Dylan's grip loosens. I swing in the air, start to slide through his arms. 'Dylan, I'm going to fall!'

He grabs tight, heaves me up, and tosses me down on the bridge. 'So. Danny,' he says, standing over me.

'Okay, okay,' Suckhole sobs. 'Danny kept trying to touch me all summer.'

'What?' Dylan turns to her.

'I wouldn't let him. It was awful.'

'Why didn't you tell me?'

'I knew you'd beat him. Then my parents would break us up. I kept quiet for you. For us. Zoe knew. She promised not to tell. Only now she's wrecked it. Forgive me?'

'Madi, hey, hey.' Dylan hugs her. 'It's not your fault.'

Katie and Caitlyn rub her shoulders: 'Oh, Madi. Madi, poor you.'

Suckhole hugs them, too. 'I'm sorry. I should have said. I didn't think you'd understand. I didn't think you'd believe me.'

'Of course we would,' Dylan says. 'You're Madi. And yeah, I would've beat the shit out of him.'

'What would I do without you?' the turdlet blossoms. She wipes her eyes and glares me. 'Okay. You tell anyone about tonight – anyone – we'll get you. Understand? You won't know where, you won't know when, but we'll stuff you in the car and finish what we started.'

I curl into a ball.

'Let's go,' Suckhole says to the others. 'The skank can walk back.'

They drive off.

20

The taillights disappear. It's so quiet I hear my heartbeat. So dark all I see are specks of light from distant farmhouses. I start to walk, trip in potholes, keep going. At the highway, I head towards town. The whole way, I flash on the rocks, the glass, the barbed wire under the bridge. It's all on Katie's phone. Me getting spit on, hanging over the bridge. I bet they're watching it right now, laughing.

Will they post it? If only: *See, Mom and Dad? Tell me I'm lying now.* Madi's too smart.

I hug my arms. I don't feel anything. Cars pass. I'm glad no one stops. They might know my folks.

I see the street lights where the highway goes into town. It must be after midnight. Nobody's around. I shiver. I don't feel cold, but I must be. The only thing I know is I stink of sweat, dirt and rum cooler. I reach the park. Home. Tomorrow, these clothes go in the trash.

I slip in through the side door. The air is heavy with hair sprays and tuna casserole. I tiptoe through the kitchen into the salon. The lights go on. Mom and Dad are sitting on the dryer chairs in their pyjamas and dressing gowns. Mom's wig is crooked. Dad's totally damp.

'Where have you been?' His voice is scary quiet.

'Nowhere.'

He gets up, a different Dad than I've ever seen. 'Where. Have. You. Been?'

'I told you. Nowhere. I couldn't sleep. I went for a walk.'

'Like that?' Mom goes.

'Booze,' Dad says. 'You stink of it.'

'No, I—'

'Who's the boy?' from Mom.

'There isn't a boy.'

'No? Just look at that dirt. Who were you rolling around with?'

'No one.'

'Then what were you doing?'

'You won't believe me.'

'We will if it's true,' Dad says.

'Fine. I was with Madi. Happy?'

'Madi? You think this is funny?'

'No. She wanted to kill me.'

'Right.' Mom heads to the phone. 'I'm calling your aunt Jess. I'm telling her what you said. You want that?'

'No! She really *will* kill me.'

'Shame on you. Shame.'

'I told you. You *never* believe me.'

'I wonder why with your condoms and drugs, that get-up.' Dad's face is a river of sweat. 'How many times have you snuck out like this?'

'Never. This is the first.'

'It's never the first!'

'You need help,' Mom goes. 'There's a doctor in Woodstock.'

'You want to stuff me with pills? Make me like Granny?'

'Honey, you're not well. We've tried everything else.'

'Yeah, right,' I holler. 'You lock me up. You take my phone. You never listen. Well, it's not my fault you had me! Not my fault Dad never left town! Not my fault we're not the Mackenzies!'

'What?' The room is one big yell.

'Shut up!' I run to the door. 'Shut up shut up shut up!'

'Come back here, young lady!' Dad goes.

'Make me!'

'If you take off, don't come back.'

'Fine.'

I slam the door behind me, run down the road to the park, and jump on a swing. I push higher and higher till I'm level with the bar. Scream till my head's inside out: 'I HATE THIS TOWN! I HATE THIS LIFE! I WISH I WAS DEAD!

A truck hurtles down Main Street towards the highway. It speeds up as it nears the park. *It's going so fast it can't stop. So fast it won't hurt!*

I fly off the swing and race to the road. As I go to jump,

I picture Granny alone at her window. I throw myself to the side. The truck flies past, horn blaring.

Oh my God. What just happened? Have I gone crazy?

I need someplace to think. To hide.

21

I sneak into Granny's backyard and let myself into the Bird House. Her curtains are closed to keep thieves from spying, so the place is pitch black. I go for the switch, but people will see light through the curtain cracks and know someone's inside. Granny has candles in the sideboard; I can hide the glow with my hand.

I follow the walls to the dining room with my fingers. The wallpaper's covered in fuzzy green flowers. They feel like caterpillars.

I freeze. What was that sound?

Nothing, dork. This isn't a movie.

I reach the sideboard and grope inside till I find candles, a holder and a box of matches. The air moves around me. My neck prickles. Someone's here.

I stop breathing. Silence.

I light the candle, turn my head – *A face! I see a face!*

Idiot! It's my reflection from Granny's glass cabinet. I'm alone.

Unless I'm not. What if somebody broke in? Some drifter? What if he's still here?

Shepton doesn't get drifters.

Then what about Suckhole? She knows it's empty. What if she brought her gang here to get wasted? What if they hid when I opened the door?

There's a bulge in the window curtains. I put down the candle and grab the umbrella by the table.

'Suckhole, you hiding behind the curtains?'

Like she'd answer. No, she'll wait till Dylan blocks my way out the back. Then she'll jump me and—

I attack the curtains, whacking them over and over. Nobody's there.

So what? It doesn't mean they're not somewhere else.

Umbrella in one hand, candle in the other, I make my way through the living room, kitchen and study. Nothing. I'm too scared to go into the basement. Instead, I prop a chair against the door. If Suckhole comes up, I'll hear it topple.

I go upstairs and check the walk-in closets on my hands and knees so I can see feet hiding behind Granny's dresses. There aren't any. I go the bathroom and throw back the shower curtain. Nobody's there, either.

I grab a towel from the linen cabinet and shower with the door open: Granny wants to see where she is; I want to make sure nobody's sneaking up the stairs. I dry off, go back to Granny's room, and push a wooden chest in front of the door. If anyone tries to break in, I'll jump out the window.

Granny's got nighties in her chest-of-drawers from when she was heavier. They smell like mothballs. I slip one on and crawl into bed. The sheets are new, but Granny's scent comes up through the pillow covers: stale lavender, rose and talcum powder. I picture her in bed at Greenview: 'Where am I? What's going on? Why wasn't I informed?'

Don't be scared, Granny. I'll fix things. Promise.

I start to hurt from where I fell on the gravel. There's a bump on the back of my head; it must have bounced against the bridge. I listen to the creaks of the house; the party in the walls. Mice? Rats?

Is somebody there? Why do I see those movies?

I close my eyes. Open them right away. Close. Open. Close. Open. No way I can sleep. I stare at the candle on the night table. It's where the family photos used to be. It's where they *should* be. It's where they'll never be again.

Uncle Teddy! His photo! Sorry, Granny. I forgot to get you another.

I get up and pull out a row of musty cardboard boxes from under the bed. When I was little, we searched them for Dad and Uncle Teddy's toys. We went through her boxes of albums, too.

I take off the lids. The first three have board games, hand puppets, marbles, a baseball mitt and a Magic 8 ball. The fourth has albums of Granny and Grampa from when they were kids. The fifth has their wedding photos, plus pictures of them dancing, bowling, having picnics.

Fifty years from now will somebody see me in a random shot and wonder who I was?

I open the sixth. Yes! On top is an album labelled *The Boys* along with a bundle of letters to Granny held together by an elastic band.

The return addresses are from Toronto. The sender is T. Bird.

22

Life before texts and emails. Wow. I start with the earliest postmark. Ghosts fly up from the paper.

```
Dear Mom,
   I've been phoning ever since I got back
to residence, but Pop keeps hanging up.
So - I'm sorry I wrecked Christmas. I
know we wanted to visit Grandpa, but I
had to get out of the Bird House and
home to university.
   You say Pop doesn't hate me. Well he
does. I see how he looks at you and
Timmy. I want that look so bad. But I'm
me.
   Call me when you're alone.
```

Love,
Teddy

Weird. I don't remember Grampa mean. He was frail on the comfy couch. Granny stroked his forehead. He tossed me peanuts. I was his little chipmunk.

I open the next letter. It's March. Granny's visited. Uncle Teddy's sent tonnes of photos. The best is of them in the scarves Granny told me about: orange and yellow with purple sunbursts, down to their knees! From now on, I don't want Pop's help with anything, he says. I don't want to owe him anything. I'll get by with my scholarship, shiftwork and student loan, I'll be fine.

He signs them all 'Me' which is kind of fun.

More photos in the next letters. It's his second year at university and he's sharing in a house with three friends: Bruce Izumi, Lincoln 'Linc' Edwards and Susan Munroe. His best friend, Linc, has a dog called Mr Binks. Uncle Teddy looks so cool; curly hair pulled back in a ponytail; eyes as big as Bambi's.

No pictures in the next one.

Dear Mom,

You all moving to the Bird House is a good idea. Grandpa can't cope without Grandma. Sorry, but I won't ever be back. With Pop, there's no way. Let's just see each other here.

Susan says when you visit in June, she'll make a cheesecake in your honour. I'll remind her to grease the pan this

```
time. Tell Timmy I'm not like Pop
says.
```

Love,

Me

I skim over a bunch of letters, all after Granny's visits. It looks like she saw him three or four times a year. No more photos, as if they'd been there/done that, or maybe Granny's stashed them somewhere else. Anyway, Uncle Teddy never talks about Grampa, but he mentions Dad: `Timmy's little. He'll understand when he's older.`

There're just four letters left – and a new address. The first has a snapshot overlooking a park that stretches behind a strip of low-rise shops and restaurants. A park! Yes! Granny talked about him having a place across from a park! So she *does* know where he lives! Or lived.

```
Hey Mom,
   This is the view from my balcony.
Amazing, isn't it? I loved sharing the
house, but it's great to be on my own.
I'm still fixing up the inside. You'll
see it when you're here.
```

Love,

Me

Next letter:

> Enough with the guilt trip, Mother. I know it wasn't about me. But it wasn't about you and Pop, either. If you didn't want me there, fine, but don't pretend it was my fault.

What's that about? The next letter's a week later:

> You're upset? You think I'm not? You made a choice. Well so have I. My friends are more family than you.

Oh my gosh! Uncle Teddy disowned Granny? I shake all over.

His last letter's been ripped open and sealed with Scotch Tape. I open it up. Hundreds of bits of paper fall out.

What did Uncle Teddy write? Why did Granny rip it up and keep the pieces?

I sweep the bits of paper back into the envelope, bury the letters back in their box and lie in bed: Granny . . . Uncle Teddy . . . Uncle Teddy . . . Granny . . . Grampa . . . Mom and Dad . . . me . . . me and them . . . me and Suckhole . . . me and . . .

It's night. I'm running through a snow storm. Who's chasing me? I don't know. Their faces are covered in scarves. I get to

the bridge. They push me off. I grab at a scarf. Suckhole laughs.
It unravels – there's no one there – I'm falling—

I sit bolt upright. Light filters through the crack in the curtains. It must be Sunday morning. Ow. I'm *so* sore. And hungry.

I go to the kitchen. The cupboards are empty, but Mom and Aunt Jess missed the fig biscuits at the back of the top shelf of the pantry. I soak a couple under the tap till they're soft enough to chew, then go back to Granny's room.

What now? I can't stay here, but how do I face Mom and Dad?

The front door opens. 'Zoe?'

It's them.

23

'There's no sense hiding, Zoe,' Mom calls out. 'We'll find you.'

Oh yeah? I roll under the bed with the letters and pull the boxes in front of me, while my parents prowl around downstairs.

'Come on out,' from Dad. 'We love you. We're worried about you.'

Who's the liar now?

Doors bang open and shut.

'Tim, what's the lawn mower doing in the broom closet?'

'You tell me.'

More rummaging. They pull back furniture.

'I should never have said she couldn't come back,' Dad says.

'She knows you didn't mean it.'

'Does she? If anything happens—'

'Nothing's happened. For all we know, she slept in the park. Or maybe she's with that boy.'

'Or maybe she's gone.'

'Relax,' Mom says from the kitchen. 'There's water in the sink. She's here. Let's look upstairs.'

They come up. The floorboards creak outside Granny's bedroom.

'Zoe, you get out here now,' Mom says. 'Enough of the silly games.'

Silly games? This is silly *games?*

'We're not angry,' Dad goes. 'We're upset, but we're not angry.'

Yeah. Until you see me.

'I'll block the stairs, while you check the rooms,' Mom says.

'Fine.' Dad roots around like the Incredible Hulk, if the Incredible Hulk said stuff like, 'Holy moly, there's mouse poops under the vanity!'

They come into the bedroom. Granny's hope chest opens and shuts. Hangers clatter. I smell Mom's perfume. She's looking under the bed.

'It's nothing but boxes under there,' Dad says.

Mom pokes at them anyway. They push tight against me. She grunts, stands up, and plops her butt on the bed. The metal slats press down hard along my body. Dad sits beside her. There's a tiny crack between the boxes. I see his left shoe. They catch their breaths.

'She must've run out the back when we pulled up,' Mom says.

Dad undoes his laces; I smell his feet. 'Should we call the police?'

'No. She'll come home when she's hungry.'

'How do you know?'

'What else is she going to do?'

'Who knows? Teddy never came back.'

'Well, Teddy didn't vanish, either,' Mom says. 'Or do too badly, what with that condo. Morning coffees looking over a park. That's the life.'

So he's still in his place by the park!

'Teddy.' Dad rocks back and forth; the slats roll down over me. 'I should've given Teddy's number to Mother.'

What?

'Not this again,' Mom sighs.

'I mean it, Carrie. Things might have been different.'

'The past is the past.'

Dad breathes deep. 'The past is for ever.'

Oh my gosh. How long have they had it?

'Enough about Teddy,' Mom says. 'We need to think about Zoe. That boarding school.'

Dad stops rocking. 'You wanted that shop so much.'

'Yes, well . . . The school's her last chance. A mortgage on the house will cover the first school year. After that, we can talk to Jess and Chad.'

'I hate asking them.'

'You think I don't? Anyway, time for church. Folks'll be wondering what's keeping us.'

'What do we say if they ask about Zoe?'

'She has a cold.' Mom pats Dad's back. 'Zoe's fine, Tim. She was here till just now. She'll come home. Relax.'

They go downstairs. The front door closes. I get out from under the bed and shake my hands to get the tingles out.

I'll come home? And get shipped away to that school? I can't. Granny'll think I abandoned her. She'll forget who I am. She'll die in Greenview! What'll I do? Where can I hide?

Uncle Teddy's! I'll go to Uncle Teddy's. He's still by the park. His address is on his letters.

Why would he want me?

'Cause he'll understand. He was picked on, beaten by people, blamed for things. It won't be just me, either. I'll have Granny.

Woah! I can't take Granny.

I have to or she'll never get out of Greenview. Once she's with Uncle Teddy, my parents won't get her back.

He doesn't want to see her.

Oh yeah? On what planet does Uncle Teddy give Dad his number?

Planet Nowhere.

Right. Uncle Teddy sent Granny his number in case she wanted to call. But Dad picked up the letter. He has it: she doesn't: he said so himself. That's the only way it makes sense. No wonder Dad feels guilty. He's kept Granny and Uncle Teddy apart. Well, not any more.

24

I toss some Depends, clothes, Uncle Teddy's letters and photos into a suitcase, leave it by the front door, and run home for Granny's car keys. By the time my parents are back from church, we'll be in Woodstock on the train to Toronto.

I get to the Bensons', our neighbours on the other side of the highway. *What if they see me?* Get real. Sundays, they're wasted till noon. Besides, nobody knows I'm missing.

I run across and slip in the front door, my heart thumping up my throat. The quiet inside the house is creepy: it's like Mom and Dad can hear me. I tiptoe to their room and get Granny's keys from Dad's old cufflinks box in his bottom dresser drawer. I see my phone. I'm itching to take it, but leave it behind: can't risk the cops tracking it.

I check the train schedule on my computer. The one on Sunday leaves Woodstock in an hour and a half. Tight, but we can make it. I change into jeans and a hoodie, stuff undies and toiletries in my backpack, then go to the fridge where I fill a doubled plastic bag with cheese, bread, chips, Oreos, two Cokes and some paper towels.

I forge a note for Greenview on Mom's notepaper.

Carrie's House of Hair
Have We Got A 'Do For You!
#10078 Highway 8
519 – 676 – 0942

Dear Amy,
   Zoe will be signing Grace out of Greenview
for Sunday dinner. Tim and I will have her
back by eight o'clock this evening.

                              Yours very truly,
                              Carrie Bird

I write another for Mom and Dad which I leave in the
medicine cabinet, so they won't see it till bedtime:

Granny and I are fine. We're going where we'll never
embarrass you again.

                                          Zoe

Okay. Goodbye green bathtub. Goodbye owl clock.
Goodbye hair dryers. I close my eyes and breathe in peppermint foot scrub, potpourri, and henna. I picture Mom
fixing her wig, Dad taking off his shoes.
   Shivers. Time to spring Granny.

I put the groceries in the garbage pail at the Greenview

parking lot so Amy won't get suspicious, then run happily to her desk.

'Amy! Guess what? Mom and Dad are having Granny for dinner!'

'Oh, she'll enjoy that.'

'I hope so. I've come to get her.' I give her my note. 'Hey, great sweater.'

Amy sets it aside. 'Thank you.'

Off the elevator, I head straight to Granny's room. She's slumped in a chair staring into space, bags packed by the garden gnome.

'Rhubarb, Granny. Pie,' I say, grabbing her toothbrush. 'Let's go. We're off to Uncle Teddy's.'

Granny jumps up. 'About time! Help me with my stuff.'

'We can't take anything. If anyone thinks you're escaping, you'll be stuck here for ever. Trust me. Just smile, nod, and let me do the talking.'

Granny grips my arm. 'Lead the way, Detective Bird.'

We march down the corridor, eyes focused on the exit door beyond the recreation room. We pass the nurses' station and the wheelchairs at the TV. I tap in the code. The door opens. We take the elevator downstairs.

'I hear this is an important day,' Amy smiles at Granny as I sign us out.

'It certainly is,' Granny says. 'I'm going to see my son.'

'Enjoy yourself. We'll see you back at eight.'

'Oh you will, will you?'

I wink at Amy, scoot Granny outside, and get our groceries out of the garbage pail.

Granny looks in the bin. 'Anything else worth taking?'

'Not today.' I whisk us to Malcolm Street. 'Now hurry. We have to be out of town before Mom and Dad get home from church.'

'Why? Where are we going?'

'Uncle Teddy's.'

'About time.' She grips my arm. 'Zoe, when I die, will you look after my bird nests? I don't want them thrown out. My box with the robin eggs, too.'

'I'll look after everything, Granny. But right now, we need to speed up.'

Granny walks faster. 'Things are memories. I'm so afraid of losing my memories. If you don't have your memories, what's the point?'

We turn onto Maple, get to the Bird House, go up to the verandah.

'Would you like to have a swing?'

'Not now.' I get us inside. 'I need you to concentrate: where's your money stash?'

Her eyes narrow. 'The less you know, the less your parents have to find out.'

'I know, but we need it. Now. To pay for the train tickets to Uncle Teddy's.'

'Oh. Well, in that case.' Granny closes her eyes. 'Don't

tell me. I can practically see it. I check it all the time. What's the name of that place where I sleep?'

'The bedroom?'

'No. The thing, you know, the thing you lie on. What's the name of it?'

'The bed?'

'No. Not the bed. The other one.'

'The comfy couch?'

Granny's eyes pop open. 'That's it. It's in the comfy couch.'

She marches into the den, reaches into the hole at the back, and pulls out an old pair of pantyhose filled with money. 'Count it. There's lots.'

'Mom thinks that hole was made by a squirrel,' I say, as I add it up.

Granny snorts. 'You mean your mother can't tell the difference between a squirrel and a rat?'

'That hole was made by a rat?!?'

'Your Grampa dropped peanut shells on the floor. What'd you expect?'

'Granny. You put money in a rat's nest?'

She looks at me like I'm stupid. 'Floorboards and mattresses are the first place people look. Put it behind something, how do you remember where? But a rat's nest – that's not something you forget.'

'Granny, a rat could *eat* this!'

'Well, he's not there now, for Pete's sake. Do you think I'm crazy?' She holds out her hand. 'So how much?'

'Four hundred and change,' I put the money back in the pantyhose and hand it over.

Granny puts it in her purse. 'Told you there was lots.'

I glance at my watch. 'There's just forty-five minutes till the train leaves. We have to go.'

'No kidding we have to go. At least I do.' She scoots to the powder room, starts humming Elvis and pees and pees. *Like, wow.* The toilet flushes. The sink runs. Granny comes out wiping her hands on her track pants. 'Why, Zoe! What's the magic word?'

'We're going to be late.'

'Late?' She blinks. 'Then what are we standing around for?'

I grab the suitcase I packed her, plus the groceries and my backpack, and hurry us outside. Granny hops in the car, while I toss our stuff in the trunk.

'Where to?' she asks as I hand her the keys.

'The train station in Woodstock.'

Granny rubs her thumbs on the steering wheel. 'I don't think I drive on the highway.'

'You used to.'

'No. Your grampa drove.'

'That was before he got sick. Then you drove all the time. Come on, it'll be empty. It's Sunday morning.'

She shakes her head. 'I'm not sure.'

'But you're the one who said you'd drive!'

'I must have been joking.'

'Granny, remember when I was little, you told me the story of the little engine that could. Are you telling me you're not as good as that little engine?'

She thinks hard. 'If you put it that way. But you have to tell me what to do.'

'I promise.'

We lurch onto the street. Granny makes all the turns to the highway without me having to say a word. She drives past my place: our car's still gone. She drives past the park, the town sign – we're into the country.

This is actually going to work.

25

Granny doesn't drive any faster when we hit the country. It'd be quicker if I pushed.

'Could we speed up a bit?'

Granny presses on the gas. We head towards the ditch.

'Granny!' I point to the road.

She gets us back in our lane and we carry on, not exactly flying, but fast enough if you're not in a hurry. Which we are.

We pass the turnoff to the bridge. *Think Bird Turd can fly?*

We come up to a tractor pulling a wagonload of pumpkins. Granny slows down. Soon there's a line of cars behind us.

'Granny, everybody's waiting for us to pass.'

'Let them wait.'

'There's no one coming. We can do it easy.'

The car behind pulls out. So does Granny. The car behind brakes. Granny wobbles between our lane and the passing lane. Cars honk. Granny pulls *all* the way out. Other cars follow. Only she hardly speeds up. We inch up along the wagon. There's a hill ahead. The dotted line ends.

'Granny! Faster!' –

'I'm going as fast as I can.'

A car speeds over the hill. The tractor slows for Granny to pass – but Granny slows too!

'WE'RE GOING TO DIE!'

Granny blinks – jams her foot on the accelerator – and we fly past and into our lane as the oncoming car swerves onto the gravel. Everyone's fists are on their horns.

We're at the top of the hill. A cop car rounds the bend. Did he hear the noise? Is he slowing down?

'Granny, the farm on our right. Pull off the road. Pretend it's home.'

She does. The tractor and cars drive on as if nothing's happened. The cop keeps going.

'Well,' Granny says, 'that's enough driving for me today.'

You think? But we're still ten minutes from Woodstock.

'Granny, I'm going to ask that farmhouse to call us a cab, okay?' I take the keys so she won't drive off without me.

A woman answers the door. She's holding a bottle of Windex and a cleaning rag, her hair's in a kerchief.

I point to Granny's car. 'Sorry to bother you, but my granny and I have had car trouble and my phone's dead. Could I please use yours? We need a taxi to Woodstock.'

She sees Granny waving. 'Come in. Sorry about the mess.' She brings me to the landline in the kitchen. There's a Woodstock Taxi magnet on the fridge.

I make the call. 'We'll have one there for you in ten minutes,' the guy says. Good. Add another ten minutes to get to the station and that still gives us ten before the train leaves.

'Will you be wanting a tow truck?' the woman asks.

'I'll have Dad get one when he's back from church.'

'Sounds good. I'll keep an eye out for you. If you and your grandmother would like to wait inside . . .'

'No, that's fine, thanks.'

I go back to the highway and get our stuff out of the trunk. Cars pass. More cars pass.

What if there's someone we know? What if they call Mom and Dad?

I check the time. It's been ten minutes since I called. Eleven minutes. I kick at the gravel. Twelve minutes. Thirteen. Fourteen. *Where's the taxi? We're running out of time!?*

A camper comes over the hill. *That means a young family or seniors, right? It's safe to hitchhike, right!?!*

'Granny! Make like we're in trouble! 'Cause we are!'

Granny waves her arms like a majorette while I step onto the road, hands up, eyes pleading: *Please! Help! I'm a poor girl with her granny!*

The camper pulls over. It's got Kentucky licence plates. There's an old couple inside. He's got an *I've Been To Disney World* T-shirt; she's in a polka-dot dress and straw hat.

'You folks in trouble?' the man asks.

'We sure are,' I say. 'We were going to Woodstock, but our car broke down. My parents aren't answering the phone and we need a ride.'

'Hop in. Tell us where to.'

'Thanks. It's the next town ahead, maybe ten minutes.'

Granny and I settle into the back seat with our things.

'We're Hal and Bette Perkins,' the man says – and boy do Hal and Bette Perkins like to talk. They have three kids and seven grandkids, and they've been travelling around North America since Hal retired two years ago from being an accountant for a shingle company in Louisville.

'We always had the itch to travel, but never the time,' Mr Perkins says. 'Now we can't get enough of it. Oh, the stories this trailer could tell. I once found a man's false teeth in a restroom in Oregon.'

'Is that a fact?' Granny says brightly. 'I once saw a man expose himself.'

'Pardon?' Mrs Perkins says, like she didn't hear right.

'I was five or six in the candy aisle at Kresge's.'

'Good Heavens. What did your parents say?'

'Can't say as I told them. But it made an impression. First time I'd seen one of those things.'

'I guess there's a first time for everything,' Mrs Perkins says politely.

'A last time, too,' Granny laughs. 'Which reminds me of a joke.' *Oh no.* 'Why is our church stuck with a piano?'

'Why?'

'Because Pastor Nolan keeps the organ in his pants!'

'Sooo,' I interrupt, 'we're coming into Woodstock. Keep straight along the railroad tracks.'

'I have another joke!' Granny has a million. She started telling them at church, which is why Mom and Dad stopped bringing her.

'Granny, I'm trying to give Mr Perkins directions.'

'Well, it's a doozy, but you go ahead.'

'Okay, turn right at the crossover to the train station,' I say to the Perkins. 'We can walk from there easy.'

'Nonsense,' Mrs Perkins says, as we cross over. 'We'll drop you right at your door.'

'It's there,' I point to the house on the corner.

'My, you *are* close,' Mr Perkins says.

'What's happening?' Granny asks as I get us out of the car.

'We're saying goodbye to Mr and Mrs Perkins.'

Granny shakes Mrs Perkins' hand through the open window. 'It was so good to see you again.'

They wave us goodbye and drive off. There's a long whistle as the train pulls in.

'Quick, Granny.' We run for all we're worth, throw open the station door and race to the wicket. Granny fumbles me money. I grab our tickets. 'Wait!' I call to the porter as he goes to pull up the foot step.

We hop aboard. As we take our seats, the train pulls out of the station.

26

Finally. I can breathe. No one knows who we are or where we're going.

'I'm hungry,' Granny says.

'Not to worry.' I hand her some bread and cheese from the grocery bag. 'For dessert, there's Oreos.'

'You should open a restaurant.' Granny stares at her food for a bit, then wraps it in a Kleenex and slips it into her coat pocket. Not me. After my cheese sandwich, I have the bag of chips and six cookies.

'Granny . . . when was the last time you saw Uncle Teddy?'

'Oh . . . a while back.'

'How long is a while back?'

'Time's funny, Pumpkin. At my age, everything goes by so fast it's hard to tell.' She pinches the skin on the back of her hands. It stays up. 'See? That's what happens when you get old.'

'You're not that old.'

'Old enough I bet you can't imagine I climbed trees.'

'You climbed the tree beside the Methodist church where you grew up,' I grin. 'There was a branch that went over

131

the roof. You hopped onto it and they had to call a fire truck to get you down.'

Granny laughs. 'How do you know so much?'

'I listen.'

'And I talk. Aren't we the pair?' She looks surprised. 'I have to tinkle.'

I take Granny's arm and lead her to the bathroom. She steadies herself on the door frame while I line the toilet seat with paper. It's a habit Mom taught me when I was little. She took me to a restaurant stall and made a nest with half a roll, like we were there to hatch eggs. 'You don't know who's been sitting here,' she said. I pictured my kindergarten teacher.

I've been laying paper ever since, even at home. I don't want my bum anywhere near my parents'. I get Granny seated.

'Stay,' she says.

'There's no room.'

'Please. I'll get lost trying to find you.'

'Don't worry. I'll be right outside.'

Granny chews her lip like it's beef jerky. I leave the door open a crack, stand in front, and bring her back to the seat when she's done. She glances out the window. *Does she wonder why we're here? Does she remember where we're going?*

I put my hand on hers. We smile at each other. *Everything's okay, Granny. I'm here for you. I'll take care of you. Always.*

We sit like that for a long time. A cloud crosses her face. She looks back out the window. Me too.

I'll bet there are runaways from every town we're rolling through. Were they running to something, from something: both? What happened after they left? I picture Dad looking for me, Mom at the window in those slippers that look like rabbits.

When Greenview phones, they'll call the cops. They'll find the abandoned car. Did that woman see the camper; get the licence plate?

I picture fifty squad cars screeching up to the Perkins'. *That's a better story than finding false teeth in a washroom, right, Mr Perkins? You're welcome, ha ha.*

Stop it, it's not funny. There'll be Missing Persons fliers at the laundromat. Sniffer dogs combing fields and woodlots.

So what? Nobody cared about me before. Why should I care now?

But Mom and Dad—

They'll have my note: it says we're fine.

Granny snores. I close my eyes and picture Uncle Teddy. I wonder if he'll have grey hair? A beard? He'll hug Granny, they'll cry, then I'll say, 'Can I stay with you, too?' and Granny will say, 'Please', and he'll say, 'Of course'. I wonder if he'll adopt me?

The train slows. I see the CN Tower in the distance. We pull into Union Station. People start getting their luggage off the overhead rack.

Granny wakes up. 'What's going on?'

'Nothing. We're in Toronto.'

'Toronto?'

'We caught the train after I got you out of Greenview.'

'What was I doing in Greenview?'

'Don't worry. You're never going back.'

'You can say that again. I live at the Bird House, 125 Maple Street. It's where I'm going to die, too.'

'For sure. But before that, we have to get to Uncle Teddy.'

The train lurches to a stop. Everyone fills the aisle. I put our leftovers in my backpack, get Granny's suitcase, and lead her to the exit door. Getting out of the station is tricky: the crowd rushes in all directions; Granny's distracted by the shops. Outside, my heart beats even faster. Everywhere – skyscrapers, food stands, people from all over. What a great place to hide in.

So long, Shepton. Hello life.

27

A dozen taxis are lined up at the curb. I help Granny into one and give the driver Uncle Teddy's address. He zips through lights, running a red and swerving left onto Jarvis. He tears past a bicycle.

'You almost picked the ass off that one!' Granny whoops.

I count the numbers on the buildings. We're getting close to Uncle Teddy's. There's a huge park down a cross street; it must be the one he sees from his apartment. The driver pulls up to the curb.

Wait a sec. This is it? I double-check the address. *This is it all right. Why does Mom call it a fancy condo?* Rusty air conditioners poke out of the windows; the bins by the front door spill garbage.

Never mind. I pay the driver and get Granny to the front door. She sits on her suitcase, surrounded by cigarette butts and dead gum, while I check for Uncle Teddy on the buzzer panel. Barker. Bentley. Carley.

Where's Bird? It should be before Carley.

I check again. Bentley. Carley. *Where's Uncle Teddy?* I press the superintendent's buzzer. Count to twenty. Do it again.

A voice crackles out of the speaker box; noise in the background. 'Yeah?'

'I'm looking for Teddy Bird.'

'Can't hear you – Louise, turn that damn TV down.' He and Louise yell at each other, then: 'Who do you want again?'

'Teddy Bird.'

'There's no Teddy Bird here.'

'This is the address on all his letters.'

'Not my problem.'

The speaker goes dead. I buzz again and again: he doesn't pick up.

Stomach to throat: *He* has *moved since the letters. Mom said his condo overlooks a park. She never said* this *park. There must be hundreds in Toronto. Thousands.*

Granny peers up at me. 'What's this about Teddy?'

'He's out.'

'Hah! He *pretends* to be out. He does it for spite.' She picks up her suitcase. 'Let's go. I can't think for the noise.'

I can't think period. 'How about a picnic? There's a park two minutes from here.'

'Swell.'

Granny takes my arm and I walk us across the street, past Sonny's Family Diner – '24-Hour Breakfast Special' and a block of rundown stores with apartments on top. The park doesn't look like it did from the cab. The grass is weeds, the wading pool's full of coffee cups, and guys are drinking out of paper bags.

We should go home. We can't, so breathe. I'm not the only kid who's run away. *With her grandmother?*

I get us to a free bench. Across the street, a guy on a cardboard sheet sprawls beside the front door to the E-Zee Rest Hotel. He's got a cup and a sign that says 'Free Smiles'. I try not to stare at him.

Granny puts her hands in her coat pockets, blinks, and pulls out her cheese sandwich. 'Look what I found. Want some?'

'No, thanks.' Cross fingers she doesn't see the guy peeing against the tree behind us.

Granny breaks off some bread, tosses it to a pigeon, and puts the rest of the sandwich back in her pocket.

Uncle Teddy, where are you? How do I find you?

Pigeons flap all around. 'Shoo, that was for him, not you,' Granny scolds. She glances over. 'What's wrong, Pumpkin?'

'Nothing.'

'Good.' She drumrolls her knees. 'We should be getting home.'

'Not right now.'

'Why not?'

Because, because . . . 'We're on a trip.' I point at her suitcase.

'So that's what that's doing here.' She looks around. 'You know, I have a feeling I've been here before. Something reminds me of something.'

'Maybe you visited Uncle Teddy.'

Granny shakes her head. 'No. I visited Teddy in Toronto.'

'That's where we are now.'

'Well, that explains it then.'

Granny, please be quiet. I have to think.

She fidgets. 'So where have your parents gone off to?'

'They're back home.'

Granny blinks. 'What are they doing there?'

'Granny, this is hard to say, but Mom and Dad put you in Greenview.'

'What?'

'I know. So I got you out. And we ran away. Only now we're in Toronto and things are falling apart only we can't go back 'cause they'll lock you back up, and I'll be in so much trouble, and I don't know what to do – I just, I just – I wish I was dead.'

'Don't ever say that. Where would I be without you?'

'Oh, Granny, why do you love me? Why would anyone love me?'

'Because you're you. Don't fret. Things always turn out.'

'No, they don't.'

'Okay, they don't, but we've got each other and that's a start. Have a Kleenex.' She reaches into her pocket and pulls out her sandwich. 'Why, look what I found.' I laugh despite myself. Granny laughs, too. 'I think you're just tired. We should have a lie-down.'

I look across the street at the E-Zee Rest Hotel. We have to stay somewhere. At least it looks cheap.

The man on the cardboard by the entrance has a rumpled suit with a toothbrush in the jacket pocket. 'Free smiles.'

'Thank you.' Granny gives him a smile back. We go inside.

The lobby smells of air freshener and bug spray. The lights are low; I'm guessing that's a good thing. The woman at the reception desk looks like a prison guard. 'Can I help you?'

'Maybe.' Granny turns to me. 'Are we here for a room?' I nod. 'We're here for a room.'

'How long will you be staying?'

'A couple of nights.' Granny reaches into her purse and pulls out the pantyhose. 'How much?'

'Two nights? Two hundred and forty, plus tax,' the receptionist says like she sees this every day. 'Do you have a credit card?'

'Sorry,' I say.

The receptionist gives us the once-over. 'Guess you're not likely to trash the place.' She takes Granny's cash and gives her a registration form.

Granny squints. 'My glasses are acting up. How about you deal with this, Pumpkin.'

I write: Madi and Emily Oiseau, 123 Rue de la Maison, Montreal.

The receptionist hands me the swipe key. 'Room 304. Enjoy your stay.'

28

Room 304 is like the lobby, only smaller as in just-enough-room-to-turn-round smaller. The carpet's a grubby brown check, there's black stuff growing between the bathroom tiles and the window looks over a sketchy alley. At least it's not the street.

Yeah, well, we'll be there soon if I don't find Uncle Teddy. After the hotel, train and cab, we only have a hundred bucks.

'Want to watch TV?' I ask.

'Up to you,' Granny says.

I squeeze two chairs in front of the television and turn on music videos. There's so much dust on the screen I could write my name.

By now, Mom and Dad know Granny's car is missing. Mom's called Aunt Jess. Suckhole's called the Suckhole-ettes. What'll I do?

Granny frowns at the screen. 'I don't get it.'

'There's nothing to get. It's music videos.'

She shakes her head. 'I don't get it.' ·

'Fine. Pick something else.' I give her the remote.

Granny stares at it like it's a Rubik's cube. 'Are you upset, Pumpkin?'

'No. I'm trying to thinking is all.'

'Good. You go ahead and think.'

I try to concentrate, but Granny keeps smiling at me. I shut my eyes to block her out: if I was a real detective, how would I find Uncle Teddy's address?

I open my eyes. Granny's still smiling: 'How's the thinking going?'

'Just fine, Granny.'

I close my eyes again. Only what can I think? How can I think?

Granny has the rest of her sandwich for dinner. I pace back and forth along the bed, chewing Oreos.

'What are you doing?' Granny asks.

'Exercising.'

'You should try push-ups.' Granny counts my steps in each direction.

Before you know it, it's night. I get out my toothbrush and the extra I brought for Granny. 'Time to brush our teeth and go to bed, Granny.'

'I've already brushed mine.'

'No, you haven't.'

She juts her jaw. 'How would you know?'

'Because I have it right here.'

'So what? I used my finger.'

'Great,' I smile. 'Now you can use your toothbrush. I need you to show me how to brush mine properly.'

'Your parents haven't taught you?'

'Not the way you do it.'

Granny sighs and follows me into the bathroom. I give her her toothbrush and she cleans her teeth.

I tap my teeth where she missed: 'How do I do here?'

She shows me, brushing like she's scrubbing floors. I use the same trick to get her to do behind her molars. After, we go back to the bedroom. I pull back the bedcovers; there're hairs in the sheets. At this point, who cares?

Granny gets into bed with her shoes on.

'Can I help you off with those?'

Granny shakes her head. 'Someone will steal them.'

'Who?'

'You'd be surprised.'

Fine. I tuck her in, turn out the lights, and sit by the window, looking out over the alley. Down below, a guy is rooting through the dumpster. *Will that be Granny and me?* A wave of sick goes up my throat. The guy looks up. I pull back into the dark. *Who will watch me?*

I crawl into bed. Close my eyes. On the back of my eyelids I see Suckhole, Mom and Dad, the last few days. *'Think Bird Turd can fly?'*

Granny tosses and turns. In the middle of the night, she kicks me.

'Ow!'

She wakes up startled. 'Who's there?'

'Me. Zoe.'

'You should go home,' Granny says. 'Your mom and dad will be cross at me for keeping you up so late .'

'They're away for the weekend.'

'They left you alone?'

'I'm not alone. I'm with *you*. We're having a sleepover.'

'Oh, good,' Granny says. 'I like it when we have sleepovers.'

'Me too. So let's *sleep*.'

'All right.' A minute later. 'Zoe,' she says, a little concerned.

'What?'

'This doesn't feel like my bed.'

'That's 'cause it isn't.'

'Oh. So whose is it?'

Pause. 'Granny, I'm going to turn on the light. Promise you won't freak out.'

'Why would I do that?'

'Just promise. Okay?'

'Okay, promise.'

I turn on the lamp.

Granny sits bolt upright. 'Where are we?'

'In a hotel room in Toronto.'

'Toronto?' She pulls the bedcover to her chest. 'How did we get here?'

'You promised not to freak out.'

'I'm not freaking out. I'm— I don't know what.'

'Mom and Dad put you in Greenview,' I say calmly.

'You said Uncle Teddy would save you, so we ran away to find him.'

Granny looks at me like I'm crazy. 'Teddy cut me off. Dear God, why are the things I want to forget the things I remember?'

I hold Granny tight. 'Whatever happened back then, he loves you.'

'Really?'

'Really.' I stroke her hair, whisper the lullabies she used to sing me, and lay us back onto our pillows. The world disappears.

29

I'm falling. Barbed wire, rocks rush towards my head—

I open my eyes. It's morning. Granny's grinning at me from two inches away. 'Rise and shine, lazy bones. I thought you were dead.' This is a joke. I think. 'I'm already dressed. Take me wherever it is we're going.'

Breakfast would be a start. I get us to Sonny's Family Diner, opposite Uncle Teddy's old apartment. There's cracked leatherette seats and a bowl of jelly beans by the cashier. We slide into a booth at the front. Granny copies what I do with my serviette and menu.

'What would you like, Granny?'

'Whatever you're having.'

I order us breakfast specials and stare at Uncle Teddy's old building. *Where did you move? How do I find you?*

Hi My Name Is Trevor drops off our plates. Could he have cleaned his fingernails maybe? I picture the kitchen. I wish I hadn't.

Granny pokes at her eggs while I look back across the street. A couple of people leave Uncle Teddy's. *Hey, what if they lived there before he left? What if they knew him?*

'Sit still, Granny.' I run outside but they're gone.

Who cares. There's other people to try. Not everyone moves. Maybe somebody knows where he went!

I run back to our table. 'Granny, we have to go. I've got work to do.'

Once in our room, I set Granny in front of the aquarium channel, put the Uncle Teddy pictures in my knapsack, and hang a note on the doorknob: GRANNY, STAY HERE! I'LL BE BACK SOON! XOX ZOE!

'I'm just stepping out for a bit, okay?'

'Take your time,' Granny says. An angelfish crosses the screen.

I race to Uncle Teddy's. The return address on his envelope says apartment 1206, but the buzzers don't have numbers. A guy comes up behind me, smelling of cigarettes and chewing gum. I step back. A friend buzzes him in. I catch the door with my foot, wait till he catches the elevator, and sneak inside.

I smooth my hair in the smoked-mirrored wall and wipe the bacon grease off my chin. By the time the elevator arrives, I'm what Mom would call 'presentable'. I get off on the twelfth floor. 1206, is immediately on my right. For a second, I get this weird vibe like I've time travelled and he's inside doing dishes.

Uh, no. A baby's screaming its head off. I knock at the next one. 'Hold on.' A guy with a man-bun props open the door. 'Who are you?'

'Teddy Bird's niece. He used to live in 1206.' I show him a picture. 'Did you know him?'

'Hunh? No. How did you get in here?'

'Someone held the door for me.'

'You're a tailgater?'

'What? No. I'm just trying to find my uncle.'

'Or trying to find an empty apartment to break into.'

'No. Look, it's important I find him.'

'It's important you get your ass outside. You want to find someone, use the buzzer.' He slams the door.

Bite me, Man-bun. Who made you God?

There are only yappy dogs at the next two apartments, but at the third, I hear people talking a foreign language. I knock. Everything goes quiet. A woman peeks through the crack at the chain lock. 'Husband no home.'

'That's okay.' I show her my uncle's picture. 'Do you know Teddy Bird?'

'Husband no home. No home.'

I nod and talk slowly: 'I Know I'm Looking For Teddy Bird.'

'You go now. Shoo.' She locks the door and I'm alone again in the hall.

Drip marks trail from the next apartment to the garbage chute down the hall. I knock. Shuffling. The door opens. The windows have heavy shades across them. The air is thick as plum jelly; it smells of cat litter.

The man in the shadows has a cane. A faded nightgown hangs open over underwear, pale, hairless legs, and fuzzy slippers. Cats circle his feet. 'I've been waiting for you.'

'Uh, I don't think so. I'm looking for my uncle. He used to live on this floor.'

'I've lived here for thirty-six years.'

'His name is Teddy Bird.' I hold up the picture. 'Did you know him?'

'Maybe.' He hardly looks at it. 'Come in.' His eyes are big.

'That's okay.' I shift back and forth. 'I wonder, could you please check if his name's in your address book?'

'Of course. Come in while I look for it.'

'I don't want to bother you.'

'You won't bother me. I have cats. Want to pet my cats?'

The elevator opens behind me. Out comes a bald guy tough as a tractor; his arms are hairier than Mom's wig. 'You the tailgater?' He takes my photo with his phone. 'You the one who broke into 504, 912?'

'No, I— Who are you anyway?'

'The superintendent. Who are you?'

'This is my granddaughter,' the man in the shadows says.

The superintendent shoots him a hard look. 'You have a lot of granddaughters, Mr McCutcheon.'

'Don't worry about him,' the man in shadows purrs. 'Come in.'

'I'd love to, Grampa, but I'm late for school.'

'Come by later then. Grampa has a present for you.' He winks. My heart somersaults.

The superintendent presses the elevator button. I ride down with him.

'It's not like you think,' I go. 'I'm the one who buzzed you yesterday about my uncle, Teddy Bird. He lived here. I have to find him.'

'That's not my problem. You are.' The elevator opens. He marches me to the front door. 'If I see you in this building again, I'll call the cops.'

I walk back and forth in front of the building. He can't stop me from talking to people, can he? I run after a woman who leaves with a dog; up to a man coming home with a gym bag. They've never heard of Uncle Teddy.

What have I done?

I wonder what Mom and Dad are thinking? I wonder, I wonder, I wonder—

What have I done?

I stop the mailman. He doesn't recognise the name. Couldn't tell me if he did.

What have I done?

I stop a man coming back with a case of beer and a woman with a cart of laundry. They never knew Uncle Teddy, either. Neither does anyone else.

I slump on the stoop. *Uncle Teddy, what happens if I don't find you?* I fall through my insides.

WHAT HAVE I DONE!

30

I spend hours more chasing people. Back home, Dad'll be scratching his arches. Mom'll be poking at her wig. I used to laugh. Not now.

A police car stops across the street. *Did someone report me?* The cop gets out. I turn my head and walk down the street. *Is he crossing?* I'm scared to look. I run. I picture him after me – closer, closer.

My lungs rip up my throat. I circle the block to the E-Zee Rest. Look back for the cop. He's not there. *Was he ever?* I catch my breath, hands on knees. Even Dad doesn't sweat this much.

'Free Smiles,' says the man on the pavement. His eyes are milky; his face is dough. 'You remind me of Kimberley. My daughter.' He reaches into his pocket and pulls out the kind of snapshot you'd have in your wallet. 'She's going to be a ballet dancer.' Kimberley's maybe five, in a tutu, waving a wand.

'She's very sweet.' I sound surprised; I don't mean to.

'Thank you.' He stares at the picture.

I hesitate. 'Do you see her?'

'No,' he says, 'but I will.'

How long have you been out here? Why? Instead: 'I have to go see Granny.'

'Give her a smile for me.'

'I will – and here's one for you.'

I step into the hotel. No one's at reception. Granny's on one of the leatherette couches in the lobby: head back, mouth open, snoring. Her suitcase is beside her, her purse slung over her shoulder. My note's under her hand.

'Granny, wake up.'

Her head jerks. 'Hunh?'

'Why are you in the lobby? You can't wander like that.'

'I didn't wander. You wandered. I've been sleeping.'

'You were supposed to stay in the room. See that note in your hand?'

Granny glances down. 'It says, "Stay here". That's where I am. Here.'

'Never mind.' I take her suitcase to the elevator. She follows. We ride up to the room, me going crazy: *what if Granny'd disappeared?*

I stick the swipe key in our lock; the light goes red. I try again. Same thing. Great. 'We need a new key.' Down we go to the front desk. The receptionist's still on a break. I ding the bell for service.

'My great-grandfather had wooden teeth,' Granny says out of nowhere.

I'm about to ding again when the receptionist comes out of the room behind the desk. 'May I help you?'

'Yes, please. Our key doesn't work.'

'Your grandmother checked out an hour ago,' the receptionist says.

'Granny?'

'Don't look at me,' Granny says.

'Granny made a mistake,' I tell the receptionist.

'Did I now?' Granny says, like I haven't a clue.

'Yes, Granny, we're staying at least another night.'

The receptionist hands me a new registration form. 'That will be one hundred and twenty dollars plus tax.'

Granny opens her purse. I see the receipt from checkout. I count the money in her pantyhose.

'Where's the refund you gave her?' I ask the receptionist.

'I wouldn't know,' she says with an RBF.

'Like hell. You took it.'

'Lower your voice. Your grandmother initialled the receipt.'

'I don't care what she initialled. She didn't read it.'

'How do you know?' Granny snaps.

'Either way, it doesn't matter,' the receptionist says. 'If you want a room, it's a hundred and twenty dollars plus tax, cash or credit.'

'You can't just take our money. Give us the key or I'll call the cops.'

'Be my guest. I'll have you charged with disturbing the peace. Trespassing.'

'You wouldn't.'

The receptionist turns to Granny. 'How long have you lived in Montreal, Mrs Bird?'

Granny wrinkles her nose. 'I don't live in Montreal. I live at 125 Maple Street, Shepton, Ontario.'

The receptionist nods at the guest phone. 'Go ahead, *Miss Oiseau*. Call the police. I'm sure you have nothing to hide.'

31

We leave in a hurry. I need a smile but the man on the
cardboard is asleep. Granny squeezes her knees.

'What's wrong?'

'I have to tinkle.'

'Why didn't you go inside?'

'I didn't have to then. I sure do now.'

I hurry us to Sonny's Diner. The women's is locked.
The men's too. Granny shifts from foot to foot. *Hi My
Name Is Trevor* is texting behind the cash register. 'I need
the key to the bathroom.'

'Restrooms are for customers only.'

'We were customers this morning.'

'That was this morning.'

'Fine. Get us some fries at the booth by the window
and give me the key.' *Plus, smell your pits. There's a new
invention called soap. You should try it sometime.*

He hands me a key attached to a ping-pong paddle. I
get Granny into the bathroom. She's already dropping her
pants. I turn to go.

'Stay!' she says. 'I won't know where I am.'

'Okay.' I lean against the sink and check the graffiti by the towel dispenser.

There's an awful smell. 'Zoe, I need your help.'

I turn. Granny looks between me and the Depends around her ankles. She didn't make it in time. For anything.

'What do I do?' Granny whispers. 'Mother will be so angry.'

I kneel beside her, outside my body. 'She won't mind.'

'But what will I tell her?'

'We all have accidents. Remember how you used to change me?'

'But what do I do *now*?' Granny pleads. 'I should know this. I *do* know this. But what's the order?'

I pat her knee. 'Everything's going to be fine. Nobody's going to know.'

Stay calm. I can't let Granny see I'm scared. 'First, I'm going to take off your shoes. Then I'm going to slip your feet out of your pants and onto your shoes so they won't get dirty. Okay?'

'Okay.'

And that's what I do, one foot at a time. I separate the Depends from her track pants with paper towels and put them in the sanitary disposal. Some stuff got on the pants; I set the pants on the sink for later.

'Okay, Granny, now I'm going to give you paper towels

155

to wipe off the worst of it. Then I'll hand you ones with soap for you to scrub. All right?'

She looks at me so trusting. 'All right.'

I do the same for the rinse and the drying. Every so often she looks up at me to make sure she's doing it right. 'Excellent,' I say like she said to me when I was little.

There's a knock on the door. 'How much longer?' from the woman outside.

'I don't know. A year?'

I get a new Depends and a skirt from the suitcase. Granny wrinkles her nose when I put her feet through the leg holes of the Depends. 'What's this?'

'Your new underwear.'

'It looks like a diaper. I want my old underwear.'

'I got it for you special. See the cushiony seat? It's to keep your bum from hurting when you sit.'

'Well, if you got it special,' Granny says.

She lets me dress her, then watches me wash the seat of her track pants in the sink. I roll them up, top to bottom to keep the outside dry, and put them back in the suitcase.

Another knock. 'I'm still waiting,' from the woman.

'So use the men's.' Honestly. 'Time to wash your hands, Granny.'

She does. 'Your grampa only washed his hands in the morning and before he read the Bible. "Waste not, want not," he used to say, even for toilet water. If it had been up to him we'd have only flushed once a week.'

Flushing! I almost forget. I go to press the lever, but whoops. Granny dropped her paper towels into the toilet. *Well, I'm not going to pull them out, am I?* I flush. The towels disappear. Water rises up the bowl. It stops at the rim and settles down slowly. Whew.

We step outside. The woman waiting makes a face.

'You crap roses?' I hand the key to *Hi My Name Is Trevor* and get Granny back to our booth. The fries are cold. I pound out half a bottle of ketchup.

There's a scream from the bathroom. The woman runs out shrieking. Apparently Granny and I plugged the toilet and when she flushed, it flooded. Big deal. You'd think she had to swim through a sewer.

'It was fine when we left,' I call out.

Trevor glares at us anyway, grabs a mop and puts up an *Out of Order* sign.

The rest of the afternoon, Granny and I use the men's. We go every few hours: you can't be too careful. I bring her suitcase so it won't get stolen, but I leave my hoodie to hold our table.

Trevor keeps asking if we've finished our fries.

'Not yet.' *Not ever. We're moving in, Trev.*

I wish that was funny. *Well, it isn't. But where are we going to stay after tonight?* I don't know. *That's not an answer.* Shut up shut up shut up.

It gets dark. *Hi My Name Is Trevor* turns into *Hi My Name Is Harold*. He's Dad's age with arms so hairy you could stuff sofas. The crowd changes, too. The girls are skinny with grey skin. The guys have scars.

'I'm bored,' Granny says out of nowhere.

'Me too. Want to look at some pictures?' I pull the photos of Uncle Teddy and his friends from my knapsack.

Granny gasps. 'Where did these come from?'

'Under your bed.'

She touches his face, lost in the picture. 'Teddy had such nice friends. Look at them all, curled up like kittens.'

'Grampa wouldn't have liked that.'

'He didn't like much. Hard as a mule and twice as stupid. I loved him anyway.' She taps the photograph. 'That was Teddy's best friend. He did card tricks.'

'Granny . . . was Uncle Teddy gay?'

She shakes her head.

''Cause I wouldn't mind.'

'Well, neither would I,' she says.

'Good. But if it wasn't that, why did the two of you stop talking?'

'Why ask me? I didn't stop.' Her eyes dart like squirrels. 'I'm getting out of here, Miss Nosy. I'm going home.' She slides out of the booth.

'Granny, wait. I'm taking you out for dinner.'

'No. You're driving me crazy.' She heads to the door.

I catch her. 'Granny. Uncle Teddy. His photos are on the table.'

'My Heavens!' She runs back to the booth, slides into

her seat, and sweeps them up like she's rescuing babies. Her eyes lock on the one on top. 'Look at those curls. What lovely curls. Your grampa cut them.'

'What? When he was grown up?'

'Of course not. When he was little.' She hands me the photo. It's of Uncle Teddy and friends decorating a Christmas tree. 'Those were his housemates,' Granny says. 'Lincoln "Linc" Edwards. Bruce Izumi. Susan Munroe.'

My jaw drops. 'How do you remember their names?'

'They're written on the back.'

D'uh, I knew that. There's names on the back of every photo. 'I wonder what happened to them?'

Granny shrugs. 'Likely some moved, some stayed.'

'Oh my gosh, yes! Some stayed. Yes!' My brain goes electric. 'Why don't we see what's under our nose?'

'I give up. Why don't we see what's under our nose?'

'Tomorrow we're going to a library.'

'Hunh?' Granny makes a face. 'What kind of riddle is that?'

'It's not a riddle. I'm going to google these names; trace the ones still living in Toronto.'

'If you say so.' She blinks. 'I'm tired.'

I roll my hoodie into a ball. 'Rest your head on this.'

Granny leans against the end of the booth, the hoodie propped on her shoulder. 'Sweet dreams, Pumpkin.' Her eyes close.

No dreams for me. I'm too excited. Tomorrow, I'll track down Uncle Teddy. I just need to get us through the night.

32

It's after midnight. The place is empty, except for two guys passing paper bags under the table and a gnarly woman in sweaters. Outside, a man missing an ear presses his face to the window and knocks on the glass. I pretend I'm invisible. Granny wakes up and waves. He yells at her and lurches down the street.

'What's his problem?' Granny says.

The druggies leave. The old woman stuffs her pockets with ketchup packets and shuffles off with her pushcart.

'Everyone seems to be going,' Granny says. 'We should go, too.'

'But I'm taking you out for dinner.'

'Why, how nice.'

A car drops off a guy of maybe seventeen, eighteen. He saunters inside and up to the counter. His jeans are so tight you can practically see everything.

'Toasted Western and fries.' His voice is butter.

The Guy sits at a table, facing us. I sneak peeks, playing with my fork. He knows it, too. I want to crawl under the table. He smiles.

Look away! I can't. *So hide in the bathroom.*

'Granny, do you have to go to the washroom?'

'As a matter of fact, I do.'

I walk Granny and her suitcase past the Guy's table. He has green eyes, dirty blond hair, and the sweetest kiss curls ever. The tattoo on his neck is feathers. I force my eyeballs to look at *Hi My Name Is Harold*, AKA Mr Happy-Not. 'We need the key again.' He hands it to me like some dungeon master.

I wait till I think the Guy will've gone, but when we come out he's still eating his Western. Meanwhile, our leftovers have been cleared and Mr Happy-Not's wiping our table.

'What do you think you're doing?'

'This isn't a shelter,' Mr Happy-Not goes.

'You threw out our fries.'

'Give me a break.'

'No, you give *her* a break.' It's him. The Guy.

'Mind your own business,' from Mr Happy-Not.

'Come on, Harold.' The Guy pulls a few bucks from his pocket. 'Get them two chocolate milkshakes and a burger. Keep the change.'

Mr Happy-Not growls off to give our order to the kitchen. The Guy tosses me a wink as I get Granny back to our table.

'Aren't you going to say thank you?' Granny whispers.

'I don't know him.'

'For Heaven's sake, you can be polite without tossing

161

your legs in the air.' She turns and hollers: 'My grand-daughter Zoe would like to say thank you.'

'Granny!'

'You're welcome, Zoe.' The Guy slouches down. 'Care to join me?'

'She'd be delighted,' Granny says, 'but don't you try anything. I'll be watching.' She gives him the fingers-eyes sign.

If I was redder I'd be a tomato. The Guy switches sides as I sit at his table, facing Granny. Two skinheads come in and take the booth across from us.

'You just get into town?' the Guy asks quietly.

'No. We're waiting to take the train out.'

'Most people wait at the station.'

'We aren't most people. My father's driving us there.'

'Why isn't he here?'

'We came from shopping.'

'Stores closed hours ago. Besides, who shops with a suitcase?'

'People who don't like being bothered by strangers.'

He leans in. 'You think you're tough? You're not. You need to ditch your grandmother. Drop her off at a hospital or a shelter.'

'What?'

'She'll never make it on the streets, and she'll take you down with her.'

A woman twitches through the door in torn pantyhose

and a skirt that barely covers her ass. 'C-coffee. Yeah. Coffee.' She sits somewhere behind us.

'We're not on the street,' I say. 'I have an uncle.'

'Sure. Like your "father".'

'No. I also have the names of his friends. I just need to track them down.'

The Guy runs a hand through his hair. 'Look, if you want, you can stay at my place tonight. It's a hole but you'll be safe.'

'You want me and Granny to go with you?'

'One night. That's it. I'm not a babysitter.'

'Right. Like, I'm really going to go home with a stranger. I know exactly what guys like you are after.'

'Oh yeah?' he snorts. 'I'm not into girls.' *Do I ever feel stupid.* He hunches in. 'Here's the deal, princess. That meth head has her eye on your grandmother's suitcase. The skinheads over there have their eye on you. When I leave, Harold'll kick you out. You want what comes next?'

I gulp. 'You're just scaring me, right?'

His phone beeps. 'Work. My place is on the way. Coming or not?'

'I don't know. I— What's your name?'

'Ryder Knight.'

'Your *real* name.'

'You ask too many questions.' Ryder slides out of the booth. 'Don't say I didn't offer.' He heads out the door.

I glance at the skinheads. They're staring through my

top. One of them licks a finger. 'Granny quick' – I run to our table – 'we have to move it.'

'What?'

I grab her suitcase and hustle us out the door. 'Ryder, wait up!'

33

Ryder takes us along side streets full of weeds and sagging porches. A lot of the houses are boarded up. Others have windows covered in tinfoil and duct tape.

'Are we getting near the Bird House?' Granny asks.

'Not tonight. We're staying at our friend's place.'

Ryder flicks on a pocket flashlight and leads us up a lane of tilted garages.

I stop. 'Where are you taking us?'

'My place.'

Granny tugs at my sleeve. 'What's going on?'

'It's okay, Granny.' I call to Ryder: 'We're going back.'

He rolls a garage door part way up. 'It's just through here.'

What happens if we follow him? What happens if we don't?

Ryder disappears into the garage. There could be people inside ready to jump us. *I want to be home.* I hold Granny's hand as we dip our heads into the dark. Overhead, things run along the rafters.

'Rats,' Granny says. 'I've told your grampa we need traps.'

Ryder opens the far door to the yards of a five-unit

rowhouse. The doors and windows are nailed over with sheets of plywood and big *No Trespassing* signs. The roof in the middle is caved-in.

'There's no electricity or water,' Ryder says. 'If you have to go, squat behind the junk pile. I've got a bucket in my room, but only for emergencies.'

'You mean this is your place?'

'It beats the street.'

Okay, yeah. 'Granny, do you have to go to the bathroom?'

She makes a squeeze sound. 'No. I'm good.'

We cross piles of junk to a rotting deck; a clothes line runs from the door above to the telephone pole by the garage. We duck under the deck and take four stairs down to a sheet of plywood leaning against the wall. Ryder wedges it to the side. Behind, there's an open doorway to a basement.

We go inside. Eyes gleam at us out of the dark. Ryder shoots his light at a family of raccoons. The mother shakes herself and slouches them next door through a hole in the shared wall. Ryder pulls the plywood back into place.

'This is like a dream I have,' Granny says, as we follow his light up the stairs. 'I walk through dark rooms and I don't know where I am. Is this that dream?'

'Yes, but I'm here and it has a happy ending.'

'Good.'

At the top of the stairs is a kitchen lit by a kerosene lamp. A man is raking the walls. We walk down a hall of graffiti.

'Who else lives here?' I whisper to Ryder.

'Depends on the night. I have a lock on my door and a bolt inside. I've only been broken-in to twice.'

We stop at a door with crowbar marks on the frame. Ryder unlocks a padlock and we step inside. A mattress and sleeping bag are flopped in the middle of the room. Clothes are heaped on shelves of plywood and cinder blocks. There's a table with candles and matches, a duffel bag in the corner, empty pizza boxes and pop cans on the floor.

Ryder lights the candle. 'Don't worry about the mattress. I've slept on it for six months, haven't been bitten yet.'

'Where did it come from?' *The dump?*

'It belonged to the girl before me; a Laura, Lanie, somebody. She got on the wrong side of the Razor on George Street. Disappeared. Anyway, lock up. I'll be back by morning.' He takes off.

Wait! My throat's frozen. I bolt the door.

'So, where are we?' Granny puzzles. 'Still in that dream?'

'At a friend's place.'

'Oh.' She pokes her nose around.

I look at the bed. *Did Laura/Lanie run away like me? Is this a dead girl's mattress?*

Granny shakes out the sleeping bag and crawls underneath. 'Sorry, I can't keep my eyes open.'

'Granny, first let me take off your shoes. Please? You've had them on for a few days.'

'So? I don't want cold feet. Your grampa had cold feet. Gave him pneumonia. That's what killed him. Cold feet.' She yawns. 'Nighty night. Turn off the light on your way out.' And she's asleep.

I snuff the candle and cuddle beside her. *Running away. What was I thinking?*

A bunch of people crash up the stairs. There's yelling in the kitchen. Crazy talk. Whoever it is bangs their way down the hall. I pull the sleeping bag over our heads to hide. They stumble up to the second floor.

How long before morning?

34

Light pierces a crack in the plywood over the window. Granny's still asleep. She mumbled crazy stuff all night. I know 'cause I was awake. My skin's clammy. I'm chilled to the bone. There's nowhere to run. I wipe my eyes.

Normal Tuesdays, I'd be finishing breakfast, Mom would be making her grocery list and Dad'd be talking back at the phone-in show. *What are they doing today? Are Granny and I in the news? If only I had my phone.*

A knock. 'It's me. Ryder.'

I let him in. He's smaller than I remembered. His face is bruised. He takes off his shirt. More bruises.

'What happened?'

'Guess.' He swipes on some deodorant.

'It's from that "job", isn't it?'

'What do you care?'

'Do you do what I think you do?'

He slips into a cotton sweater. 'Probably.'

Granny rubs her eyes. 'What's the commotion?'

'Ryder's back,' I say. 'He let us stay here last night.'

'I'm taking you guys to Trigger and Tibet's,' Ryder says.

169

'They're friends of mine. They have a guest room and a toilet.'

'Great idea,' Granny says. 'I have to go pretty bad.' She squints at Ryder. 'Did you fall down the stairs?'

'Sure.'

We're dressed from yesterday, so we head out right away. Granny can't wait for Trigger and Tibet's. She does her business behind the junk pile while Ryder and I stand lookout.

'Can I borrow your phone?' I ask. 'Please? I have to check a few things online.'

Ryder passes it to me. I google 'Zoe Bird' + 'Grace Bird' and get six hits; all local radio stations and newspapers. The *Free Press* says we're missing: we called a cab from the Blackstock Farm and disappeared; anyone with information is asked to call police. Luckily, Granny's photo is blurred; mine's from a yearbook.

'You done?' Ryder asks me, as Granny comes back from the tyres.

'Yeah. Sure.' I hand him his phone.

Ryder leads us back towards the restaurant. Past the park, we stop at a shop: 2TZ Tattoos. I look between the bars over the window. Up front there's a counter; in the middle, couches held together by gaffer tape; at the back, two barbershop chairs with tray carts. The walls are covered in coffins and swords.

'Relax,' Ryder says. 'The Ts raised twins over the shop.'

He opens the door. Instead of a tinkling bell, there's a scream. A tall, skinny, bald woman swings round on one of the barbershop chairs. She's somewhere between Mom's age and Granny's, ears rimmed with rings, arms and scalp with ghosts and Buddhas.

'Hey, Trigger,' she calls upstairs, 'come see what the tide washed in.' So she's Tibet. Her face changes as she gets closer. 'Whoa, not again.'

Trigger rolls down into the shop, an apple in a bandana. 'Oh man.' He stares at the bruising.

'It's no big deal,' Ryder says.

'Tell that to the mirror. You're gonna get yourself killed.'

'I won't be working the street for ever.'

'That's what you said two years ago.'

'Preach much? You haven't even asked about my friends.'

Tibet's forehead wrinkles up onto her scalp. 'Sorry,' she says to Granny and me. 'You are . . . ?'

'Zoe Bird. And this is my granny, Grace Bird.'

'Pleased to meet you,' Granny says, and shakes their hands.

'I found them last night at Sonny's, took them home,' Ryder says.

'Aw, kiddo.' Tibet hugs me, voice like a blanket, hands like work gloves. 'It's rough, hunh?' She opens her arms for Granny.

Granny's eyebrows pop up. 'Who died?'

'Nobody, Granny. We're at a tattoo shop.'

171

Granny blinks. 'My cousin had a tattoo on his back. Big one from the war. When he passed away, they put it in a picture frame. The rest of him got cremated.'

'They skinned his back?'

'It was his last request. Raised a few eyebrows. My aunt kept it hidden in a closet.'

'Where did it end up?' Trigger smiles.

'Garage sale, maybe? I have to tinkle.'

Again?

Tibet brings Granny and me to the upstairs bathroom and heads back down. Okay, so Granny was fibbing. This time it isn't to 'tinkle'. She concentrates like for a math exam. A really hard math exam. Finally—

Plop.

Pause. 'So are you done?'

'No,' Granny shakes her head. 'He has a friend.'

I snort. 'What's his name?'

'Junior.'

Plop.

We laugh. I help her wash up. When we step out, I hear arguing downstairs.

'I don't have room,' Ryder says.

'So you thought you'd dump them on us?'

'You've helped before.'

'Since when are favours expectations?'

'I didn't know it was such a big deal.'

'Quit with the bullshit, buster,' Tibet explodes. 'You

thought you'd waltz in with that poor kid and her grandma, and we'd be stuck while you'd play hero. Well, I'm too damn old to play den mother.'

'I can hear you,' I call down.

Awkward silence.

I turn to Granny. 'Stay here a minute? I'll be right back.' I sit her in a chair by a skull lamp and head down to the shop. Trigger and Tibet are hunched in the barbershop chairs. Ryder's staring at the floor like a kid reamed out by teachers.

'Granny and I don't want a place to stay,' I say. 'All we want is my uncle. He and Granny had a fight. They stopped talking. He's somewhere in the city, only I don't know where. I just need to find him, to get them back together.'

'The city's a big place,' Trigger says.

'Zoe?' Granny calls from upstairs. 'Zoe, where are you?'

'Right here, Granny,' I call back. 'I'll be up in a sec.' I look back at the Ts. 'I have the names of his friends but I don't have a phone. If I can stay here a few hours, try to find them on the computer, make a few calls – that's all I need. Promise.'

'Zoe?' Granny calls. 'Zoe, where are you?'

'Right here. Don't worry. I'm coming up.'

I give a last look at Tibet. She thinks hard, twisting her snake ring. 'There's an old computer in the twins' room,' she says. 'I can lend you my mobile. We'll toss in lunch and a shower. But six o'clock, when we close . . .'

'Got it. Thanks.'

'Zoe?'

'I. Said. I'm. Coming. Granny!'

35

Ryder leaves. Granny and I have porridge and toast. After, Tibet logs me onto the computer in the twins' room. Downstairs, Trigger revs his tatt gun.

'I better get to work,' Tibet says. 'It can get crazy with just one of us on the floor.' She hands me her phone. 'Good luck.'

Granny sits on the lower bunk. I pass her photos of Uncle Teddy. Bruce Izumi, Lincoln 'Linc' Edwards, and Susan Munroe: those were his housemates. I start by searching his best friend, Linc. Canada411 has two L. Edwards.

Granny taps my chair back. 'What's the magic word?'

'Rhubarb,' I say, as I phone the first.

'Pie!'

'Granny, I need to concentrate.'

A few more rings. 'Hello?'

'Hi. I'm looking for a Linc Edwards.'

'Sorry. I'm Leslie.' Click.

Granny taps my chair back. 'What's the magic word?'

'RHUBARB! PIE! I'M CONCENTRATING!'

'Sorry, Pumpkin.' It's like I've slapped her face.

'Oh, Granny.' I squeeze her hand. 'I love playing Detective Bird, but can we do it "in a while, crocodile"?'

'Okay,' Granny curls up on the bed: 'See you later, alligator.' Her eyes close and her mouth falls open.

I try the second Edwards.

'We're not in. You know what to do. Beep.'

The voice is way too young, but I leave a message anyway. Then I check S. Monroes. There's a Sam, Sandra, Sarah, Seth and a bunch of others, but for all I know she moved or got married and changed her name. This is impossible.

Shut up. It can't be.

I try Izumi. *Yes!* Bruce Izumi. 248 Hiawatha Road. I dial. A woman picks up: 'Hello?'

'Hi. This is Zoe Bird. Could I please speak to Bruce?'

Heartbeat. 'I'm afraid Bruce passed away last year.'

'What? Pardon? Gosh. I'm sorry. I'm . . .' I see a young Bruce Izumi smiling into Uncle Teddy's camera. *He's dead?*

'Is there something I can help you with?'

'I don't know. I— Your husband shared a house in university with Linc Edwards, Susan Munroe and Teddy Bird.'

'I don't recall Teddy, but I met the others.'

'My uncle moved. Do you have Susan and Linc's phone numbers?'

'Sorry, no,' the woman says. 'I think Linc's a lawyer downtown somewhere.'

176

'Thanks for the tip. About your husband – I'm very sorry.'

'Thank you. Good luck finding your uncle.' She hangs up.

I click Toronto Businesses. Go to lawyers. Scroll down and – there's his name. His last name anyway. I dial the firm.

'Dunphy, Edwards and Holmes,' the receptionist says. I picture her like in the movies with high cheekbones and perfect skin.

I try and sound like an adult. 'Could I please speak to Mr Edwards?'

'I'm afraid he's busy,' she says. 'May I take a message?'

'Uh, no, it's personal. It's about a close friend. Teddy Bird. He's died.'

'I'm so sorry. Your name?'

'Zoe Bird.'

'One moment please.' Muzak.

A man comes on the line; he has a light Jamaican accent. 'Linc Edwards. Has something happened to Teddy?'

'No. I told your receptionist he was dead, but that was so I could talk to you.'

'I beg your pardon?'

'I'm Zoe Bird, Teddy's niece, only I don't think he knows I exist. I'm in town with my grandmother, his mom. Do you have his number?'

Pause. 'What does Mrs Bird want?'

'Nothing. Look, this isn't a scam, okay? I've read Uncle Teddy's letters and I know you were his friend and you shared a house with Bruce Izumi and Susan Munroe, and had a dog called Mr Binks and do card tricks and, well – Granny needs Uncle Teddy's help.'

'If you've read the letters, you'll know they stopped talking.'

'Yes. Only Granny's sorry. Really sorry. And nobody's perfect, right?' I choke up.

'Zoe . . . Did I get the name right? Zoe?'

'Yes.'

His voice goes kind, which makes it worse: 'Zoe, you're young, so I know this is hard to hear, but sometimes things are best left alone.'

'Not this time . . .' *Get the words out. Granny needs me to get the words out.* 'I'm all Granny's got. And I'm not enough. I want to be, but I'm not. She needs help. If I don't find Uncle Teddy, she'll be locked up in a home. I love her . . . Please.'

Silence. Then: 'What's your number?'

'416–268–4952. Only it's not my number. It's the number of Tibet somebody, she runs 2TZ Tattoos near his old apartment on Jarvis. Anyway, Granny and I will only be here till six tonight. Then we'll be on the street or in shelters or I don't know where.' My voice catches.

'I'll pass on your information,' Mr Edwards says. 'That's all I can do.'

'All right. Thank you.'

The line goes dead.

Okay, he's calling Uncle Teddy now . . . Uncle Teddy's calling back . . .

I stare at the phone. Nothing.

Fine, so he had to think about it. He's calling now.

Still nothing.

NOW!!! . . . Come on . . . Uncle Teddy, what kind of person are you? You know your mom and me are on the streets. And you can't even pick up the phone? You don't even have the guts to tell us to drop dead? What kind of creep are you?

No, he's not a creep. Mr Edwards hasn't reached him, that's all. He's on the phone with somebody else. I just need to wait; to not think about it.

How? I know. It's been days since Granny's shoes were off. I'll air out her feet.

I gently remove her shoes and pull back her socks. Specks of dead skin line the black cotton like snowflakes. My heart flutters. I go to the bathroom, bring back a bottle of skin cream and rub in the lotion. Granny's breath is a light whistle. I put on fresh socks and cover her feet with a blanket.

Uncle Teddy still hasn't called.

There has to be a reason. Pastor Nolan says there's a reason for everything.

What if there isn't?

I get a wave of homesickness. Mom's gals will be hanging

round the dinette set, waiting for news. I hear Mom's – 'I'm not worried' – while she wonders how long till they find our bodies. Later, she'll sit alone, wiping her hands, while Dad cuts the grass to keep his mind off things.

A lump bubbles up my throat. I should call them. *I can't.* I have to. *No.* Air – I need air. I write, Granny, stay upstairs. ☺ Zoe on two sheets of paper. I tuck one inside Granny's left shoe, and take the other downstairs.

Trigger's working on a guy who's covered in tatts of passport stamps. Tibet's got a woman squeezing a tennis ball.

'Granny's sleeping. I'm going outside for some private time. If she comes down, can you show her this note?'

'Uh-huh.' Their tatt guns sound like dentist drills.

I put it on Tibet's tray and step outside. The door screams like I feel. The sky's clouding over. I sit on the pavement under the window bars and bang my head against the bricks. *I can't go home. Not now. But if Uncle Teddy doesn't call, I'll have to send Granny back. Ryder's right: she'll get sick or hurt out here.*

I bang my head again. *Granny, I'm going to take you to a hospital. I'll give them Mom and Dad's number. They'll bring you home . . . No, I can't go with you. I have to stay here . . . No, you can't stay with me. I'm sorry. I have to say goodbye.*

I bang my head again. *Uncle Teddy, call. Please call.*

Like magic, the phone rings. There's no caller ID. 'Yeah.'

'I'm looking for Zoe Bird.' It's some woman.

'That's me.'

'I understand that you and your grandmother are at 2TZ tattoo shop and you're trying to reach your uncle.'

'Yes. Uncle Teddy.'

'Can you be at the Tim Horton's, 150 Jarvis Street in an hour?'

Heart flip. 'You bet.'

I alert Trigger and Tibet. 'Good luck,' they shout as I run out the door to the coffee shop. It's, like, only five minutes away. I get a table for two by a window and stress away the time staring at every middle-aged man coming through the door, crossing the street, walking up the sidewalk, even. *Is it him? Him? Him? Will he be bald? Have a beard? What if he has a family and kids? What if he hasn't got room for us?*

The clouds are darker. Specks of rain spit against my window. A woman comes in wearing a navy dress suit with matching cream shoulder bag and shoes. A bit overdressed for a place like this. She collapses her umbrella, looks around, and marches to my table. 'Zoe Bird?'

'Says who? I haven't done anything.'

'No?'

All of a sudden it hits me: The curls. The upturned nose. The cheekbones.

'Uncle Teddy?'

36

'Teddi, yes, with an "i". Uncle, not so much.' She sits. 'I'm not what you were expecting?'

'No. Yes. I mean, I don't know what I was expecting.'

'That's okay. There was no need to tell you.'

Ohmigod ohmigod ohmigod. Act normal. 'I tried to find you online.'

'I changed my last name to Burgess.'

'Burgess?'

'My husband's name.' She taps the table. 'You look like you need a doughnut.'

'I'm not hungry.'

'I am.' She gets up. 'Sit tight.'

So my uncle – my aunt? – is trans? And married?

I watch her at the cash register: crisp, no-nonsense. Her hair and make-up aren't like the gals at Mom's salon: the curls are short and she's light on the liner. Not much jewelry, either; just a plain silver necklace and a wedding ring. Her hands are big. Nice nails.

Teddi comes back with two honey glazes, a coffee for her, a Coke for me, and serviettes.

'Thank you.'

She nods. The smile drops. 'So. What are you doing with my mother in Toronto? At a tattoo shop?'

'Please don't yell at me.'

'I'm not yelling. I'm asking.'

I wrap my feet round the chair legs. 'Okay. Well. I don't know how to say it, I mean I do but it would take for ever, so forget about me. Granny. My parents put Granny in a nursing home, and she doesn't want to be there, like *really* doesn't want to be there – she says she'll die. And she says you'd never have done that, you'd take care of her, so I got her out and we've been trying to find you ever since.'

'I see.' Teddi cuts her doughnut in half and has a bite. 'First, your granny's not going to die from being in a care home. Second, she doesn't need *my* help. She needs help period. She can't manage any more.'

'How would you know?'

'Your dad phoned last night, worried sick. He wondered if you'd contacted me. I understand my name's come up in conversation.'

'Don't believe anything he told you. If it weren't for him, you'd be with Granny.'

'Your father has nothing to do with what happened between your granny and me.'

'That's what you think. When you mailed Granny your new phone number, Dad stole the letter. That's why she never wrote or called you.'

Teddi taps her lips with a napkin. 'I never sent your granny anything.'

'Then how did Dad know where to reach you?'

'He's known for years. I made contact with him when he was twenty. He asked if I wanted to visit. I said no, I didn't want to open old wounds, but would he pass on the news when our parents died. He was good enough to call about your grandfather.'

I'm drowning. Pull me up. Somebody.

Teddi puts her hand on my arm. 'Your dad's a nice guy, Zoe. I can tell.'

There's a hole where my stomach should be: 'Do they know you found me?'

She nods. 'I said we were going to meet, then I'd call and they could come to pick you up.'

'What? No!'

Thunder in the distance.

'Zoe,' Teddi says calmly. 'I know you care about your granny, but I'm not your happy ending.'

'You can't decide that till you talk to her.'

'We haven't talked for thirty years. We're strangers.'

'You're not thirty years ago to Granny. You're now.'

'Yes. Well.' Teddi glances at the rain trickling down the window.

'You loved each other.'

'Very much.'

I search her face. 'How can a person love someone so much they can't see them any more?'

'You'll understand when it happens. For your sake, I hope it doesn't.'

'Please. I'm sorry, it's just . . .' My eyes well, my ears burn. 'Granny's all I've got. I have to know now.'

Teddi's eyes go motherly. She passes me a Kleenex from her purse. 'All right then,' she sighs at last. 'You've read my letters, so you know your grandfather and I hated each other. Your granny loved us both. She visited me in Toronto, hoping he'd come round. At the time, they thought I was gay. But end of second year, I told her I was actually trans-female; I'd had the evaluation and started hormone therapy; after graduation, I'd be saving for the operations.'

'Granny freaked out?'

Teddi shakes her head. 'She got a little teary, but said she loved me just the same. It wasn't a total surprise. I'd said things when I was little. At puberty I'd been a mess. When Mother said she was fine, a weight lifted. I'd been living as a woman with my friends. To be open with her was, well, the greatest feeling in the world.'

'Why didn't you send photos of the new you?'

'I did,' she says drily. 'I gather she didn't keep them?'

I flush. 'Granny has so many boxes. I'm sure they're in one of them.'

'It doesn't matter.'

'Good. But I don't get it. If you loved each other, wrote each other, phoned each other – why did things go so bad so fast?'

'My grandfather died.'

'Hunh?'

Teddi's face is stone. 'Mother asked me to come to the funeral as a man. I said no, that's not who I was. She said my grandfather's funeral wasn't about me. I said it wasn't about her and Pop, either. I'd be there as myself. Mother said, in that case, perhaps it was best if I didn't come at all: I hadn't been at the Bird House in years; I'd said I never wanted to again; people had stopped asking when I'd be up; why rock the boat? "Do you want the boys in town to beat your brother? You get to come and go. We have to live here."'

'It was kind of true, wasn't it?'

'It was kind of not the point. If you're part of a family. Which obviously I wasn't. Mother said I was being unreasonable. I asked why she couldn't understand what I've gone through; did she really think I was just playing dress-up? Things went downhill from there: angry letters, slammed receivers, tears. She said I was acting like a stranger. I said my friends didn't think so: they were like family, not her. A few days later a package arrived. It was a scarf I'd made her.'

'You had a matching one.'

Teddi nods. 'Maybe she was just lashing out. I don't know: I don't care. I wrote her a terrible letter; a letter to hurt her like she'd hurt me. We haven't communicated since. At this point, she wouldn't know me to see me.' Silence. 'Zoe, your granny can't make it on the street. You know that. She has to go back.'

I twist my serviette.

'You should go, too,' Teddi says gently. 'She'll be frightened when I take her. She'll need someone she trusts to keep her calm. You'll be there for her, won't you?'

I nod. *I'm not going to cry. I'm not.* 'So now what?'

She takes out her phone. 'Now you're going to talk to your mom and dad.'

'I can't.'

'You're a brave kid. You can do anything.' She dials. 'Tim, I'm with Zoe . . . Yes, she and Mother are okay . . .' Dad blubbers something. 'You're welcome . . . Certainly.' She passes me the phone.

I swallow. 'Dad?'

'Where on earth have you been?' he sobs.

'A hotel.'

'Your mother and I— we—'

'Zoe?' It's Mom on the other line.

'Mom, please stop crying. I'm fine.'

'We were so afraid, we thought—' Her voice is all over the phone. 'I can't say what we thought.'

'You're sending me to that school, aren't you?'

'We'll talk about that later. Right now, we just want you home.'

I can't think. I can't breathe. 'Whatever.' I choke.

Teddi retrieves the phone. 'Tim, Zoe's a little worked up right now . . . Yes, I'll tell her. It's raining. Could be bad. Not a safe time for you to be driving back and forth. They can stay with us overnight . . .' She hangs up. 'Your dad says to tell you they love you.'

'They don't even know me.'

'They want to.'

What do you know? I wipe my nose. 'Fine. Let's go get Granny.'

37

We step out under the awning. The rain's really coming down.

'Wilf?' Teddi says into her phone. 'Zoe and I have had the talk. We're on the way to 2TZ to pick up my mother. Expect us in forty minutes.' She hangs up.

'Granny hasn't met your husband, has she?'

'No.' Teddi opens her umbrella. 'It's quite the day for introductions.'

The rain pelts hard. I press beside Teddi for cover. Thunder rolls as we reach 2TZ. There's a crowd at the front taking shelter. Trigger's behind the counter, watching the till. He waves us to the back where Tibet's inking a biker's scalp. The biker's pressed against the chair, like he's braking for a crash. His teeth are sunk in a rubber ball.

'You must be Tibet,' Teddi says, like nothing phases her ever. 'I'm Zoe's aunt. Thanks for looking after her granny.'

'No problem.'

I look back at all the people. 'Is she upstairs?'

'I expect, if she's not down here. We showed her your note.' Tibet leans in to the biker: 'Just a little fill left. I'm cranking the iron into third, okay?'

'FURFA FURF!!!!' He passes out.

'You want a coffee? Shot of rye?' Tibet asks Teddi.

'Thanks, no. We should go once the storm settles.' Teddi looks over. 'Zoe, could you please get your grandmother?'

I head up the stairs. *What'll I say?* '*Granny, you're going back to Greenview*'?

I cross the living room to the twins' bedroom. Granny's suitcase is open, the pictures of her and Teddi scattered on the bedspread – but she's not here.

'Granny?'

Please let her be in the other bedroom.

She's not.

Don't panic.

'Granny?' I open the bathroom door. She's not here, either. 'Granny???'

I run down the stairs. 'Granny's not there.'

'What do you mean?' Teddi goes.

'I mean She's Not There!'

Tibet puts down her iron. 'She must've slipped out when the crowd came.'

Teddi freezes. 'MOM!' she cries in terror.

Breathe. 'The rain just started. She can't have gone far. We'd have passed her if she went the way we came. So, she must have gone in the direction of the park.'

Teddi and I barrel towards the crowd at the door.

'I'm going to vomit!' I yell.

They scatter. We run outside.

190

Teddi's umbrella blows inside out. She collapses it. 'Come on.'

We race to the park, shielding our faces with our arms. Lightning. Sheets of rain pound us in waves. The drains overflow. Rivers run over the curbs. Our shoes squish through lakes. I trip in a pothole. Teddi holds me.

Rain streams into my eyes. I can hardly see. 'GRANNY!?!' 'MOM?!'

The homeless press under the trees. We go from group to group, screaming for Granny. She isn't here. *Where is she?*

Suddenly, a squeal of brakes. Cars honk. Out of the chaos, I hear Granny's voice: 'ZOE! WHERE ARE YOU?'

More lightning. A tiny old woman turns in circles in the middle of the street. It's Granny.

'GRANNY! I'M COMING!'

'ZOE!' She turns to my voice.

I grab hold of her. Teddi leaps in front of us: waving her arms to ward off traffic. We make it to the bus shelter by the corner. A man's passed out at one side of the bench; we huddle on the other, Granny in the middle.

The rain clatters off the roof, but we're safe. Lamplights and headlights gleam through the wall of water running down the glass.

Granny clutches me. Her hair wild, matted, her eyes wide. 'Don't ever wander off like that again. You had me worried sick.'

'I won't, Granny. I won't.'

Teddi wraps her navy jacket round Granny's shoulders.

'Thank you.' Granny turns to see who helped her. A streetcar stops for a red. Its headlights flood Teddi's face. Granny stares hard. Her hand moves to her mouth. 'Zoe,' she whispers, 'do I know this person? I think I know this person. I'm sorry,' she says to Teddi, confused and afraid, 'do I know you?'

Teddi hesitates.

'I don't see like I used to. Or remember like I did. But somehow . . . There's something . . . Do I know you? . . . I think I know you. Who are you?'

'Teddi,' she says quietly.

Granny reaches out. She traces Teddi's face with her fingertips. 'I had a Teddi once. I loved my child so much.'

Teddi puts her hands on Granny's. 'I had a mom I loved.'

'Teddi.' Granny's eyes fill. 'Are you *my* Teddi?'

Teddi's face shatters. 'I am.' She presses Granny close.

Granny weeps. 'I did you wrong.'

'Shh. Shh.' Teddi strokes her hair. 'I wronged you, too.'

'Forgive me?'

'With all my heart. Forgive *me*?'

'Yes, yes,' Granny says. 'Teddi. I want to go home. Come home with me. I want us to go home.'

'We will,' Teddi says.

She nods at me. We fold into each other. The rest is silence.

38

There's a lull in the storm. By five thirty, we're back at 2TZ. Trigger and Tibet are getting ready to close, but seeing how cold and wet Granny is, they let us bring her upstairs for a warm bath. I support Granny's back as we lower her into the tub. She flexes her toes. 'Oh my, that feels good.'

I get to work with a wash cloth and a bar of soap. 'How's this?' I ask as I scrub her shoulders.

'A little to the left, Pumpkin.'

After, we dry her. I bring a change of clothes from the suitcase and help her get dressed, while Teddi phones Mom and Dad. 'I can't explain it over the phone, but I'll be driving them back. I'd like to stay with Mom at the Bird House for a couple of days before she gets resettled. We need to get reacquainted. That's not a problem, is it?' It is *so* not a question. 'Good. See you then.'

We come downstairs with our stuff. Trigger and Tibet have closed the shop. They're sitting with Ryder on the customer couches. I introduce Teddi to Ryder; she goes to get her car, and Granny and I take the green vinyl loveseat.

She nods like she's following everything, but I know she's pretty vagued out.

'What happens now?' Tibet asks.

'Teddi's taking us to her place. She's driving us home tomorrow.'

'You won't be needing me then,' Ryder says. 'I dropped by in case you had to find a shelter.'

'Thanks, but . . .' My voice trails off. I pick at the stuffing poking out from the duct tape on the armrest.

'Cheer up,' Trigger says. 'All's well that ends well.'

'Only it hasn't. Mom and Dad want me back, but . . .'

'No buts,' Ryder says. 'You have a mom and dad to go to.'

'You don't understand.'

'No. *You* don't understand.'

I don't argue with those eyes.

Granny leans into my ear. 'Are we at a party?'

'Sort of. A goodbye party.'

'Who's leaving?'

'Us. We're going home.'

'Oh good.'

It's awkward when you're stuck talking to people and have nothing to say. They've been so nice, but we all have these smiles like when we're waiting for someone to take our picture.

Teddi arrives. It's drizzling. We get Granny and our bags into the car. Trigger, Tibet and Ryder give me a hug.

Tibet slips a card in my hand in case I'm ever back in town.

'Want Teddi to drop you somewhere?' I ask Ryder.

He stuffs his hands in his pockets. 'Nah, I'll just hang here, thanks, wait for whatever.'

'Okay then. See ya.'

'See ya.'

But we won't, not ever, and we know it. As Teddi drives me away, I look back. Ryder's slouched against a street light, checking cars. He disappears in the mist.

Teddi drives us to the kind of Toronto you see in magazines. Her condo is off Mount Pleasant Boulevard, which is an actual name, not just from a comic book. It overlooks a park – okay, a cemetery – but if you were dead, it's the kind of place you'd want to live in.

Teddi's husband, Wilf, has a roast chicken ready. He's way shorter than Teddi with thinning hair and age spots. He shows us to the dining room overlooking the park. Like the art on the walls, the throw rugs, and the lamps on the glass side tables, the dining-room table's pretty wow: hardwood, stained ebony, with a centrepiece of flowers.

Wilf and I sit on one side, Teddi and Granny on the other. The two of them only have eyes for each other: Granny's shy, Teddi's tender. Once or twice a cloud passes Granny's face. 'I'm Teddi,' Teddi murmurs gently. 'Yes,' Granny smiles. 'Teddi.'

Wilf keeps me company. He's a retired principal, so naturally he asks me all about school, my favourite subjects, plus what I like to do in my spare time and what I want to be when I grow up. 'If I had it to do over again, I'd have stayed a teacher,' he says. 'I loved the classroom; all those young people full of ideas.' He taught science then. I bet he made it fun.

Granny's appetite picks up when we hit dessert: brownies and ice cream. Not long after, she starts to nod off. Teddi and I take her into the master bedroom and bundle her into a pair of Wilf's flannel pyjamas and woollen socks, while Wilf cleans up. I'll be sleeping in here with her tonight; Teddi and Wilf are taking the pullout in the second bedroom.

When Granny's asleep, we turn on a night light and tiptoe out to join Wilf, who's reading in the living room. He's made a pot of hot chocolate and set out a plate of cookies. Teddi sits with me on the sofa opposite.

'It's hard to see her like this,' Teddi says. 'Mom was always so strong.'

'She still is.' I stare down at my mug.

I wait for Teddi to argue or say something else to make me feel stupid. Only she doesn't.

'What are you thinking?' she asks gently.

'Nothing.' I dig my toes into the carpet. Teddi and Wilf don't say a word. *Talk. Say something.* They don't. *Okay. Fine.* 'I'm scared to go home.'

'Don't be. Your parents love you. It'll work out.'

'Easy for you to say. As soon I get home, they're shipping me off to this tough-love boarding school. Granny's mind's getting worse. She'll forget me. What happens then?'

Teddi puts her arm round me. 'Worry's a terrible thing.'

'I know. But how do I stop it? There's Granny. My cousin Madi. I mean she almost killed me and nobody cares.'

'What?'

All of a sudden, I'm spinning down a drain, going on about Suckhole and the bridge and getting spit on and almost dropped down onto the rocks and barbed wire, and how they can get me anywhere, anytime, and how next time they'll get me for good.

Wilf hands me a Kleenex. 'Have you told your parents?'

I nod. 'They don't believe me. They never believe me. Not about anything . . .' And all of a sudden I'm going on about the Dream House box and the drugs and the condoms and—

'I'll talk to them,' Teddi says.

'It won't make a difference.'

'We'll see.'

'We *won't* see. I *know*.' My voice goes all wobbly. 'I'm sorry, I can't talk any more, I just can't.' I run into the bedroom and shut the door. *Why am I so confused? Why can't I be normal? Why can't life be simple?*

I get into bed and press myself beside Granny.

Don't forget me, Granny. Please. Don't ever forget me.

39

Next morning, Wilf makes us pancakes. He's amazing.

Teddi reintroduces herself. For Granny, the reconciliation is new. She stares at Teddi all breakfast, her eyes glistening in wonder. A few times she asks, 'Teddi?' and Teddi says, 'Yes, Mom. I'm so glad you're here,' then, 'Me too,' from Granny.

When the dishes are cleared, Teddi disappears into the spare room. She rummages around and comes back with a small cardboard box, the kind that's been at the back of a closet.

'I have something for you, Mom,' Teddi says. She gives Granny the box.

'Why, thank you.' Granny puzzles as she lifts the lid. Inside is a knitted scarf, yellow and orange with bursts of purple. 'Oh my.'

'I have one the very same.'

'I remember this scarf. I loved this scarf. I thought I'd lost it for ever.'

'Lost and found,' Teddi says and kisses her forehead.

After breakfast, I help Granny get dressed. She insists on wearing her scarf. Teddi puts hers on, too, to help

Granny remember who she is. Then Teddi brings us down the elevator to her car in the garage.

What happens when we get home?

I open the door to the passenger seat for Granny. My hands are as sticky as Dad's. I get into the back.

'Are we going to the Bird House?' Granny asks.

'Would you like that?' Teddi asks back.

'Of course. It's where I live. It's where I'm going to die, too.'

'Well, you're not going to die anytime soon.'

'I should certainly hope not.'

Nice dodge.

Granny naps once we hit the highway; Teddi and I listen to her playlist; we pass tonnes of cars.

My brain itches. 'So, Teddi . . .'

'Yes?'

So that was stupid. Now I have to say something. 'Can I ask you a personal question?'

'Sure.' She turns down the music.

Three, two, one: 'When did you know you were a woman?'

Teddi smiles at me through the rear-view mirror. 'I'd say always, but I can't remember back that far.'

'But *how* did you know?'

'I just did. Same as you.'

'But I had the parts.'

Teddi nods. 'It was very upsetting.'

I think about that for a bit. 'Who did you tell first?'

'Mom. Your granny.'

'Really?!?'

'I was very little. She was tucking me into bed. I said, "Mommy, why don't I look like a girl?"'

'What did she say?'

'"Because you're a boy." I said: "I don't feel like a boy." "What do you think boys feel like?" she asked. "I don't know," I said. "Not like me."'

'Did Granny tell Grampa?'

'I'm pretty sure not. He'd have said something. Actually, Mom probably forgot about it. You know kids: "I want to be a pirate. I want to be a spaceman." Or in my case a mermaid or a princess.'

'Did you ever play princess in front of Grampa?'

'Just once. I was three or four. I got into Mom's pearls and camisole and ran into the living room screaming, "I'm Princess Linda."'

'Did he hit you?'

'No. He chased me upstairs though. I hid under the bed. He poked me out with a broom. Next day it was off to the barber's for a buzz cut. That made me angry for the longest time. Not now so much, unless I let it.'

I hesitate. 'When I read your letters, I thought maybe you were gay.'

'So did Mom and Pop.' Teddi glances at me in the rearview mirror. 'Coming out as trans is hard even now; it was worse back then. I was lucky to have a few good friends.' She smiles. 'Any more questions?'

'Well, if you're asking . . . How did you meet Wilf?'

'Hah! Skydiving.'

'Seriously?'

'I was there on a dare. He was there for his birthday.'

We go on like this for the rest of the trip. Me talking to forget what's coming; her being her. In what seems like no time we're off the 401. When we pass through Woodstock, Teddi calls Mom and Dad on speakerphone: 'We'll be there in twenty minutes.'

My chest tightens. 'Teddi, can I ask you one last thing?'

'Sure.'

'My only aunt is Aunt Jess. It would be nice to have an aunt I like. So is it okay if I call you Aunt Teddi?'

'Of course. You're my niece after all.'

'Thanks . . . Aunt Teddi.'

We pass the bridge cut-off, Dylan's farm, the park, and pull into the driveway. As we get out of the car, Mom and Dad run towards us. They hug me in a heartbeat.

'Zoe!' Mom exclaims. 'Thank God you're safe.'

Dad to Granny, 'Mom, you okay?'

'Sure thing. Are you?'

'I'm Teddi,' Aunt Teddi says to Mom. 'You're Carrie?'

'Yes,' Mom says, a bit nervous. 'We're so grateful you got them home in one piece.' She shakes Aunt Teddi's hand. *Did that just happen?* 'Please, come in for a coffee.'

'Thanks, but you'll be wanting private time, and Mom's pretty tired. Why don't you come by the Bird House tonight for supper? I can order in pizza.'

Mom's face somersaults. 'We'll bring the dishes and cutlery.'

'The Bird House.' Granny blinks. 'People will be sneaking in.'

Aunt Teddi takes her arm. 'We'd better get you back, then.'

Dad gives her the key and we wave them off. I wait for the yelling to start. It doesn't. Instead, Mom puts her arm round me as we head inside to the kitchen table.

'So about Toronto,' I say.

'We can talk about that later, we're just so relieved to have you home,' Dad says. 'And, right now, there's something else . . . Zoe, we need to know what you were doing before you ran away.'

'Whatever it was, honey, please tell us,' Mom says. 'We won't get mad. Promise.'

'Absolutely. Promise,' Dad says.

'I don't know what you're talking about.'

They exchange glances. Mom says, 'Last night we called the police to say that you and your granny had been found. We told them that you were with family and we were sorry for any trouble we'd caused.'

'The police called back this morning,' Dad goes. 'They said to bring you to the station when you got home.

There's an investigation going on. They want to ask you some questions.'

'What about?'

'You tell us. It's all we could do not to ask them. We thought if we said *anything* we might get you in even more trouble.'

'We'll stand by you, honey,' Mom says, 'but you have to let us know what's been going on. We need to be prepared.'

'I don't know anything about anything. Whatever's wrong, it's Madi. She's setting me up like she always does.'

Mom and Dad look hollowed out.

'I guess we'll find out when we're there,' Dad says, getting up like we're going to a funeral.

As we head out the door, Mom's phone rings. She checks who's calling. 'Not now, Jess,' she murmurs to herself. We pull out of the driveway and head to the police station.

I should've stayed on the streets.

40

We step into Chief Lambert's office: grey walls, vinyl floors, a computer desk, chairs, and a monitor mounted on a sidewall. The chief's a big, stocky guy with slicked-back grey hair and a smile that hardly shows.

Mom and Dad introduce us.

'I'm glad you're back in town,' he tells me.

My lips move, 'Thanks,' but my throat's too dry for the words to come out.

The chief motions us to the chairs in front of his desk. Mom and Dad sit close on either side of me. I wrap my feet round the chair legs and hunch in.

'Before you ask any questions,' Dad says, 'does Zoe need a lawyer?'

The chief pauses, like Dad's fallen into a trap. 'Why would she need a lawyer? What do you think she's done?'

'Nothing. I don't know. I was just asking,' Dad says, a bit shaky.

'Have you told your parents about the bridge?' the chief asks me.

The bridge? I feel sick. 'No. Not exactly.'

'What's this about a bridge?' Mom asks.

'Saturday night, your daughter was attacked on the bridge down McClennan Sideroad,' the chief says.

Mom and Dad go pale.

'We received a call from Zoe's principal at eight forty-five this morning,' he continues. 'A student reported seeing a video of the attack that he thought might be connected to Zoe's disappearance. We recovered it by nine thirty, at which point we called you.' His eyes lock on mine. 'Were you aware the video was being taken?'

I nod, embarrassed, ashamed.

'I need as much information as possible before I speak to your attackers. Could you tell me about the events that led to the video?'

I stare at my feet. 'My cousin Madi invited me to a surprise party for Ricky, a guy I like,' I say quietly. 'When Mom and Dad were in bed, I snuck out to her boyfriends' car. Only there wasn't a party. Madi and her friends drove me to the bridge and then, well, you know what happened.'

'Honey?' Mom says. She and Dad are frozen in their seats.

'If you could direct your attention to the monitor.' The chief starts the video.

I don't watch. I don't need to. I see every second in my head.

'What are you going to do?'

'Guess.'

Mom and Dad stiffen.

'*Spit on me. I'm a Bird Turd.*'

They each put an arm round me.

'*Think Bird Turd can fly?*'

They take a hand.

'*Drop her.*'

They squeeze so hard it hurts.

'*You tell anyone about tonight – anyone – we'll get you. Understand? You won't know where, you won't know when, but we'll stuff you in the car and finish what we started.*'

I hear new stuff. Inside the car, as they drive away. I look up. Madi is turned facing Katie and Caitlyn in the backseat. She imitates the way I cried: 'Help! Waaa! I'll die! Waaa!' They laugh and give her high fives. The video cuts out.

'Sweetheart . . .' Dad says like he's coming out of a nightmare.

'It's okay.'

'It's not okay,' from Mom. 'What they did . . . oh my God . . . my God.'

They hold me like Mom's fancy china. No, more than that. Like I'm the most precious, important thing in the world.

Mom strokes my hair with her lips. 'Honey, we should have listened. We should have asked questions. We pushed you away.'

'It's our fault,' from Dad.

'We're sorry, we're sorry,' they say, over and over.

A wave upends me. 'I'm sorry, too.'

I don't know how long we hold on to each other. All I know is, even if one day I get like Granny, I'll remember this moment as long as I live.

41

It's almost lunch by the time we head home from the police station. Mom checks her phone in the car. There are five voice messages from Aunt Jess. She and Uncle Chad are parked on the road by our place. They get out of their car as we pull in the driveway. Suckhole too; she'd been hiding in the backseat.

'What do they want?' I ask.

'I expect they've heard from the police and come to apologise,' Mom says. 'Look, Jess has brought flowers. Guess there's a first for everything.'

'You don't have to see your cousin if you don't want to,' Dad says.

'I'll have to sooner or later. May as well get it over with.'

'Don't say a word,' Mom says. 'Your dad and I will do the talking.' She turns to the Mackenzies with her biggest church smile. 'What a lovely surprise.'

Uncle Chad hasn't brought wine, but he stinks of scotch. Suckhole's grey as porridge. She can't look me in the eye.

'Zoe, we're so relieved you're home,' Aunt Jess says. She shoves the flowers at Mom. 'I left five messages, Carrie. Where were you?'

208

'Oh, out and about. My phone was turned off.'

Aunt Jess exhales. 'Good. We're so glad we got to you first.'

'What do you mean?' Dad asks innocently.

Uncle Chad shifts his weight. 'We've found out about something.' His breath could curdle milk.

'That sounds serious,' Mom says.

'Let's say it took us by surprise.'

Suckhole glances nervously at the highway.

'Well, come in then, come in. Coffee? Cookies?'

Everyone shakes their head no. We gather round the dinette set. Suckhole squeezes between Uncle Chad and Aunt Jess.

'So what did you find out about?' Dad asks.

'Uh, yes, well.' For once it's Uncle Chad who's sweating. 'Madi ran home from school this morning, scared out of her wits. The police called about ten thirty. It seems there was an incident Saturday night. Perhaps Zoe's told you?'

'Perhaps *you* could tell us,' Mom says with a thin smile.

Aunt Jess fingers her pearls. 'It's actually more like a misunderstanding, really. Everyone's fine. There needn't be a problem. But, well . . .'

'But, well, what?' Mom asks.

'Saturday evening, Madi was studying with friends. A boy asked them out. Madi called Zoe to see if she'd like to come and . . . I guess she did.'

'It seems the boy had had a little alcohol – you know

boys,' Uncle Chad says. 'Apparently, he held Zoe over a bridge. He pretended he was going to drop her. Of course he wasn't. It was just a silly prank.'

'Only it got videoed and now the police are involved,' Aunt Jess interrupts. 'They want us to bring Madi to the station this afternoon for questioning, if you can imagine. We thought we should have a talk before things get out of hand.'

We stare at them. Silence.

'Before I forget, heh, heh . . .' Uncle Chad says awkwardly, rubbing his hands like he's pitching a tractor. 'Jess and I have been thinking it over and, well, a salon on Main Street makes sense. We'd like to loan you the money.'

'It's what family is for,' Aunt Jess says cheerily.

Mom and Dad keep staring.

'Carrie? Tim?'

'We've seen the video,' Mom says, cold and calm.

Suckhole gasps. 'I beg your pardon?' from Aunt Jess.

'When you drove over, we were at the police station watching the video.'

'Did you really think you could bribe us?' Dad asks, astonished. 'Did you think we care more about a salon than our daughter?'

'We thought you'd come here to apologise. Stupid us.' Mom says. She turns to Madi. 'This isn't the first time you've hurt Zoe, is it? We've blamed Zoe for so much, but it's always been you, hasn't it? The drugs and the condoms

210

in her Dream House box: they were yours, weren't they?'

'Have you lost your mind?' Aunt Jess huffs.

Mom's eyes spear her to her chair. 'Your daughter learned from a pro, Jess. Since we were little, everything I loved you took or laughed at. You've treated my family like dirt. I let you. I thought I deserved it. Well, enough.'

Uncle Chad's neck puffs red at the collar. 'Who do you think you are?'

'The parents of a pretty terrific daughter,' Dad says.

'But the police!' Aunt Jess gasps. 'You have to help us with the police.'

'We don't have to do anything,' Mom says.

'Please, Zoe!' Suckhole squeals. 'I'm sorry for everything. The Dream House. The bridge. Everything!'

'Madi,' I say, quiet and calm, 'if you're really sorry, you'll change. If you're not, it's none of my business.'

'But you have to stop things. You have to say it was a joke; we were pretending.'

'Then you'll do the same to somebody else.'

'I won't.'

'Sorry.' I look her in the eye. 'It is what it is.'

Madi goes white. For a second she stands bug-eyed, then she sobs up a storm.

'Listen up, Carrie,' Aunt Jess says, rising from her chair like a hot-air balloon. 'All these years I've zipped my lip about your secret brother-in-law, or should I say *sister*-in-law. No way I wanted to be associated with that. But my family won't go down alone. You deal with the police or I'll tell the town about that *he-she* of yours.'

Dad leaps to his feet. 'You treat my sister with respect.'

Mom's on her feet, too. 'Teddi saved Zoe and Granny. She's more family than you've ever been, and a better woman than you'll ever *be*.'

'Now get out of our home.' Dad points to the door.

The Mackenzies shrink.

'We won't forget this,' Uncle Chad says, as they slink out.

'Neither will we.' Dad shuts the door behind them.

Through the window, I see them scurry to their car like sewer rats.

'What'll they do?' I go.

Mom brushes her hands. 'Who cares?'

42

We drive to the Bird House for dinner with dishes and cutlery. There's a bottle of Purell in Mom's purse.

Aunt Teddi greets us at the door. 'I never would have imagined the Bird House like this,' she whispers.

'We did what we could,' Mom says.

'Of course. It's a shock is all.' Aunt Teddi brings us to the dining-room table. I can tell Mom's relieved that she's put towels over the chair seats. Granny and I sit together.

'So how did you spend your day, Mother?' Dad asks.

Granny looks at Aunt Teddi. 'You tell them.'

'Well, we had a nap,' Aunt Teddi says. 'Then we went through the house and saw things. We found Tim's base-ball mitt, didn't we?'

Granny nods. 'It was hiding someplace or other, but we found it.'

'Then we found my high school diploma, an oven mitt that looks like a hippopotamus, and Tim's teddy bear,' Teddi says. 'After that, we came out to the verandah to see your bird nests.'

'I love my bird nests.'

The pizza guy shows up. Aunt Teddi pays and brings the boxes to the table. Dad says grace and we dig in.

'I love how you do your hair,' Mom says.

'Easy maintenance,' Aunt Teddi smiles.

Over pizza, they catch up on each other's lives. How Dad met Mom and how Aunt Teddi met Wilf. Their memories of having a much older/much younger sibling. They make it sound fun.

'What do you remember, Mother?' Dad asks.

'When I was a ten, I stuck my tongue on a fire hydrant.'

After we've finished eating, I bring down the album of Dad and Aunt Teddi as kids. We see the summer visits to the Bird House: Aunt Teddi on the front lawn, about age twelve, cradling Dad as a baby, and pulling him in a wagon when he was a toddler. Then we see Dad in elementary school playing with his summer friends, while Aunt Teddi, late in high school, sits arranged with Granny on the verandah glider.

Granny points at picture after picture, nodding and smiling.

See Aunt Teddi, Mom, Dad? This is Granny's home. Her life. It's where she belongs.

Granny starts to drift. 'Zoe, can you tuck me in?'

'Sure.'

We leave the table. I help her brush her teeth and coax her into her nightie and out of her shoes.

'Sing me a lullaby?' Granny asks, once I've gotten her under the covers.

I sing her the one she sang me when I was a kid. Granny fills in the words that I've forgotten. I give her a kiss on the forehead. 'See you tomorrow, Granny.'

'You too, Pumpkin.'

On the way downstairs, I hear my name.

'Zoe's a fine young woman,' Aunt Teddi says. 'I watched her with Mom.'

'Mother and Zoe are quite the pair, aren't they?'

'Not many kids could toilet their granny,' Aunt Teddi says. 'You've trained her well.'

'She uh, we uh—' Mom says, pleased and confused.

'She toiletted Mother?' Dad asks, like changing Depends is a miracle.

'Bathed her too,' Aunt Teddi says.

'Good Lord. The care workers at Greenview have a terrible time with that.'

Teddi laughs. 'Well, she's got the magic touch. Like I said, you've raised a wonderful kid.'

Okay, I'm getting embarrassed. I mean it's like I'm the Granny Whisperer or something. I clump down the stairs so they can hear me coming.

'Ah, there you are,' Mom says as I enter the dining room. 'Your Aunt Teddi's been saying wonderful things about you.'

'Uh, thanks?' I blush.

'Don't mention it.'

Mom gets up. 'Well, we should get going. Thanks again about Zoe, Grace, tonight.'

'No, thank *you*.' Teddi smiles, as we all move to the front door. 'Coming home wasn't like I'd expected. You've made me feel so welcome. And Tim, it's so good to see you all grown up.'

Dad shifts awkwardly. 'Good to see you, too. It shouldn't have taken so long. I've felt so guilty.'

'Why?' Aunt Teddi asks. 'It wasn't your fault.'

'When you contacted me, I should've told Mother.'

'I didn't want you to.'

'I should have anyway. The whole situation. I was afraid what people would think.'

'But we're together now,' Aunt Teddi says gently.

Dad nods. 'I'm so glad you're here.'

'Me too.'

For a second, they face each other, not knowing what to do. Then all at once, they hug. They hug so tight.

43

The kids at school all know why I was away. Suckhole and her gang have been suspended and charged with forcible confinement, reckless endangerment and uttering death threats. It's on the local news: their names have been withheld, but the town knows anyway.

In the hall, a couple of Suckhole's hangers-on tell Ricky it's *my* fault they're in trouble, and blame him for turning in the video.

'You mean you wouldn't have?' he tosses back. 'What kind of asshats are you?'

At lunch, Ricky comes up to my table. 'Mind if I join you?'

'Sure,' I say. 'Thanks about the video.'

'No big deal. Dylan showed it to me. I was so disgusted.' He pauses. 'So, uh, I hear you have an aunt?'

'Yes,' I go. 'And since everyone's talking, double yes, Aunt Teddi is trans.'

He blushes. 'So what's she like?'

'Terrific. She listens and she loves Granny.'

'Cool.'

This is when I know that Ricky's a friend. All friends

217

really care about is if you're happy. He's not the only one on my side. All through lunch, people come up to see how I am. I had no idea Madi had so many enemies; all these kids who sucked up to her 'cause they were afraid not to.

My teachers check in on me, too. They give me extensions, plus the principal tells me his door is always open. Like I'm actually going to visit, ha ha. Still.

So far the video isn't on YouTube. But hey, if it shows up, it's Madi who should be ashamed, not me.

I bike home after school. Tonight it's us hosting dinner and I want to help make it perfect. When I walk in the door, Mom's washing Ms Burke's hair, Mrs Carmichael is under the dryer, Ms Green and Mrs Gibson are still in line, and there's so many gals hanging round the dinette set that Mom's brought in the kitchen chairs.

Everyone welcomes me home, even the ones I hardly know except to make fun of, which I guess I won't be doing any more.

'That cousin of yours,' Mrs Green says, 'it just goes to show.'

'Thank goodness for your aunt,' from Ms Burke.

'You know about Aunt Teddi?'

'The gals were walking on eggshells from the moment I opened this morning,' Mom says. 'So I finally said, "Jess has been talking, has she?"'

'Honestly, Carrie, you make it sound like we gossip,' Mrs Gibson goes, all embarrassed.

'You gossip, Doris?' Mom teases, 'Heavens no. You just pass on interesting information.'

'Well you have to admit, it's not every day a long-lost relative shows up. We didn't know how you'd be taking it.'

Mom winks at me. 'Anyway, I said, "It's true. Now get a coffee and pull up a chair." I must say, it's the busiest day I've had at the salon in weeks.'

'Your aunt Teddi's a lifesaver,' Ms Greene tells me. 'She seems to have a great heart.'

'Her husband, too,' I go.

'She has a husband?'

I guess Mom didn't tell them everything. 'Yes, Uncle Wilf. He's a retired principal. With Aunt Teddi still working, he does all the cooking and cleaning.'

'Sounds like a keeper,' Mrs Gibson says. 'I can't get my husband to pick up his underwear.'

Mrs Carmichael wakes up from under the dryer. Her jaw drops when she sees me. 'ZOE!' she hollers, like everyone's deaf as she is. 'WELCOME HOME!'

I don't know what the gals think inside, but Mom is right. They're not just clients. They're friends.

44

As soon as the gals leave, we get ready for dinner. Dad and I bring the carpet up from the basement. Then he deals with the Hide-a-Bed and I help Mom make spaghetti sauce. Normally, we scoop it out of a bottle, but she wants to make a good impression. She's even bought Häagen-Dazs.

Dad's on his third shirt when Granny and Aunt Teddi arrive in their special scarves. I think Granny's is going to be part of her uniform. She holds up the ends for me to feel. 'Soft as a bunny, eh, Pumpkin?'

As we enter the living room, Mom flutters a hand at the sheets on the hair dryers. 'Sorry about the whatever.'

'Not at all,' Aunt Teddi says. 'What great colours.'

Dinner's pretty friendly. Even Granny's polite. After they've gone, Mom and Dad talk about how everything was so perfect. They're right, except it's Friday night. Tomorrow is Granny's last supper at the Bird House. Then, early Sunday, Aunt Teddi leaves and she'll be locked up again.

All night, I try to plan the most perfect speech to get Aunt Teddi to convince my parents to let Granny stay at the Bird House. I practise in my dreams, too. In one, I'm on the perch of an *actual* bird house; Aunt Teddi's nibbling worms. In the last, I'm a hatchling falling out of a nest. *Fly, fly.* I can't.

I wake up as I go to hit the ground. It's five o'clock.

I brush my teeth and go to the kitchen. By the time Mom and Dad wake up, I've got their coffee and porridge ready.

'Honey, you didn't have to do this,' Mom says.

'I wanted to.'

Dad raises as eyebrow. *Is this so Granny can stay at the Bird House?*

I toss him puppy eyes: *No.*

He frowns: *Because you know it's decided.*

I hand him a glass of fresh-squeezed orange juice: *I don't want to fight.*

'Thank you,' he says.

After breakfast, I bike over to Granny's. She's with Aunt Teddi beside the mannequin in the wheelbarrow. 'Why if it isn't Detective Bird!' Granny exclaims. We do our shtick.

'I see you've met Fred,' I say.

'Oh, yes,' Aunt Teddi winks. 'We've even shaken hands.'

'He used to wear suits in the front window of Tip Top Tailors,' I go. 'I think he's happier in a shower cap. In winter, we give him an old coat, don't we, Granny?'

'I guess we do.' She points at my old Tonka truck. 'Say,

will you look at that.' We wander over. I think of the mound of purple impatiens when Granny was gardening.

'I bet that made a very nice planter,' Aunt Teddi says.

'Still is,' Granny says. 'Weeds are just flowers growing in the wrong place.'

We head back to the verandah, stopping at the drain spout. 'Elves lived here when I was little,' I tell Aunt Teddi. 'They left me candies in plastic wrappers.'

'What a coincidence,' Aunt Teddi says. 'We had elves in the drain spout in Elmira, too, didn't we, Mom?'

Granny nods. 'Elves are a nuisance. They dig up the tulip bulbs.' She climbs the steps. 'Oh my, I think I should shut my eyes for a minute or two. I'll be on the comfy couch if you need me.'

'Okay.'

She goes inside. *Where will you be tomorrow, Granny? Was this your last walk around the yard? The last day you'll see the birdbaths and everything you care about?*

Aunt Teddi and I sit on the glider.

So this is it. Speech time. I sit on my hands to stop them from twitching; I cross my feet to keep them from tapping; my bum starts to rock. *Last night I had a good first sentence. What was it?* 'So anyway . . .' *Think!*

'Is this the conversation?' Aunt Teddi asks. *Hunh?* 'The conversation you want to have with me before I go back to Toronto?'

'How did you know?'

Aunt Teddi shrugs. 'Tomorrow's a big day. You want to make sure you've done everything you could. And that's good: regret is a terrible thing. So please, tell me what's in your heart.'

I take a deep breath. 'Tomorrow you go home and Granny goes back to Greenview, unless I can change my parents' minds. Remember in Toronto how I said that Granny needed to stay at the Bird House?'

Aunt Teddi nods.

'So now you're here. You can see how she loves it. What it means to her. How it's her life.'

She nods again.

Good. 'Before you said you wouldn't help 'cause Granny was from another lifetime. Only everything's changed since that. Also you and Dad: you're not best friends, but you get along.'

'Yes.'

'So tonight at dinner, could you please tell my parents how this is Granny's life and she should stay here?'

Aunt Teddi eases the glider to a stop. 'Zoe, that's a very important thing you just did. Speaking your mind. No matter what happens, you can be proud you took a stand.' *Please don't say what I think you're going to.* 'This isn't what you want to hear, but your parents are right,' she continues. 'Mom needs to be in Greenview. You know it deep inside, don't you?'

I swallow. 'But this is where she's happy.'

'You're right.'

'If she's in Greenview she'll be dying every day. How would you like it if you woke up every morning in a place you didn't remember with strangers telling you what to do?'

'I hope I'd be grateful my family cared enough to put me in a place where I was looked after. Wilf's father didn't want to be in a nursing home, either, but in the end he loved it.'

'Hooray for him: he's not Granny,' I go. 'I mean, Aunt Teddi, I know Greenview's great – the people, everything – and maybe Granny *should* be there. But who cares, if she'd rather be dead?'

'It's a matter of safety.'

'Safety isn't everything.'

'You're young,' she says.

'That doesn't mean I'm wrong. You'd have been safer if you'd lived as a man. Would that have been worth it?'

'That's different,' Aunt Teddi says. 'Where you live isn't who you are.'

'No, but taking risks to be happy is the same choice exactly. When you came out as trans, you risked your life. Not just with the surgeries, but with all the crazies who'd beat you, kill you, even. You did it because you had to, to be happy. Why doesn't happiness count for Granny?'

Teddi doesn't answer.

'I don't expect you to change your mind right away.

And maybe you won't change your mind at all,' I say quietly. 'But you're my favourite aunt. Okay, the only aunt I can stand. Please promise you'll think about what I said?'

'Okay, I'll think about it,' Aunt Teddi says carefully.

45

Tonight at the Bird House is supposed to be relaxed. Aunt Teddi went to the grocery store with Granny this afternoon and picked up some salads from the deli counter. Mom thawed a tub of chili con carne.

But for all the easy talk, my heart's on a tripwire. Granny nods and laughs a half second after everyone else. Mostly, though, she pokes at her food and winks at me. *Oh, Granny, if only you knew what's going to happen.*

I take her upstairs after dinner and get her ready for bed, while my parents and Aunt Teddi have cookies and coffee.

'You take better care of me than Mother,' Granny says as I tuck her in.

'I try.' I give her a kiss on the forehead, turn off her light and go downstairs.

'Well, it's back to Toronto tomorrow,' Aunt Teddi sighs as I rejoin the table.

'We hope you and Mother had a good visit,' Dad says.

'Yes. Thanks for giving us the time.'

'What time would you like us to take Grace back to Greenview?' Mom asks.

It's now or never. 'About Greenview.' They freeze. 'Look,

226

I promise I won't yell or do anything crazy, but please hear what I have to say.'

'I think we *have* heard,' Dad says gently.

'This is different. I wasn't honest with you before. I pretended Granny was fine. I was afraid what would happen if she wasn't. I acted like you were the bad guys because I didn't want to see the truth.'

Mom and Dad look surprised. 'Go on,' Dad says.

'What I did, running away, was awful. I put Granny at risk. The one good thing, apart from finding Aunt Teddi, is I got to see how *much* Granny needs. What I can do and what I can't.'

'Well, you can certainly do a lot,' Mom says. 'Aunt Teddi told us how you can bathe her, toilet her when she needs it – you should be proud of yourself.'

'We couldn't have done that,' Dad adds. 'Even Greenview has trouble.'

I blush, but it's true. *Okay, so how to put this:* 'The thing Granny needs most is supervision. We can't give her that at our place 'cause of the salon; there'd be too many problems. But if I was *here*—'

'Honey, that's not possible.'

'Why? Before you worried about drugs and boys. You don't any more, and I'd just be a phone call away. A two-minute drive.'

Dad shakes his head. 'Not during the day. You'll be at school.'

'Right, but that's where you'd come in. You mainly work online. Instead of our stinky basement, you could set up your office here in the big, sunny living room. Granny wouldn't be in your way. She sticks to her room, the den and the verandah. After work, you could drive us home for dinner, then we'd come back to sleep. I'd make breakfast and lunch.'

They shift uncomfortably. 'What about your grades?' Mom asks.

'Your gals have kids who work after school and on weekends. I'd basically be an overnight babysitter.'

Mom and Dad glance at each other. Neither knows what to say.

'Look,' I say calmly, 'it's not perfect – nothing is – and maybe it'll get to be too much. But right now, right here, Granny knows where she is. She doesn't at Greenview. Think how scary that must be. Plus, she doesn't wander except a block down on garbage night. If she ever did, it's a small town and her phone has GPS.'

'But the house.' Dad's breathing goes funny. 'Keeping up two properties . . . the time, the stress . . .'

Aunt Teddi clears her throat: 'I'll support whatever you think's right, Tim, but just so you know, Wilf and I are happy to arrange for maintenance and a regular cleaning crew. We can also hire extra help.'

'I appreciate the offer,' Dad says, 'but we don't need charity.'

'It's not charity. So far, you and Carrie have done everything for Mom. That isn't right. I need to help, and I have a lot to catch up on. I also want to see more of Mom. If you decide to give this a try, I'll stay with her every other weekend to give you all a break.'

'Thanks. That would be good if . . .' He pauses; frowns.

'Tim and I need to have a minute,' Mom says. She and Dad step outside onto the verandah.

What now? If I bite my nails, I'll end up chewing my arms off.

Aunt Teddi catches my eye. 'Want a cookie?'

'Not really.'

'Have one anyway.'

Mom and Dad come back five cookies later. They sit and look at each other, like they've decided on everything except who's supposed to say it. Mom clears her throat. Nothing. Dad clears his throat. Nothing.

'Fine then,' Mom says. 'Zoe. We've thought about what you had to say. And we're very pleased you didn't get angry.'

'Very pleased,' Dad agrees.

Pause. *I can hear the BUT.*

'But' – *I knew it* – 'we're not comfortable about what you're proposing.'

'Not comfortable at all,' Mom shakes her head. 'Please understand, honey, it's not because we don't trust you. It's just that you're asking a lot of yourself. More than I think you imagine.'

'On the one hand, you have a real way with your granny,' Dad says. 'It gets results and brings you both joy. On the other hand, the thought of you and your granny alone here—'

I slump. 'So it's a no.'

'That's not what we said.'

'It's what you meant. You don't want me to be here.'

'We don't want you here *alone*,' Dad says. 'But when your mom and I got talking we thought about another possibility. We haven't had time to think it through, so it may be totally crazy, but, well . . .'

'Tell me!'

'Okay, whew boy.' Dad cracks his knuckles. 'The Bird House is your granny's home. But, as you know, it's *my* home, too. It's where I lived from age seven till your mom and I got married.'

'For quite a while, we've wanted to move the salon out of the house; to get my gals out of our hair, so to speak,' Mom says. 'We've wanted a proper family home, a place you could bring friends without feeling embarrassed.'

Dad nods. 'We've been focussed on getting a store in town. But since Teddi's prepared to handle maintenance and extra help, and since you're better than Greenview at getting your granny bathed and dressed, the thought occurred to us: what if the salon stays where it is and we made our home at the Bird House?'

My brain's a dryer on spin cycle.

'We'd be counting on you to work your magic with Granny,' Mom says. 'She may not want me anywhere near the place. She's been quite harsh.'

'Granny likes you fine, Mom. She just doesn't like when you boss her.'

Mom sits back in her chair. 'I don't boss her.'

'Well, not boss maybe, but she's sure heard you say she can't live how she's living. The idea of being forced out of her home scares her to death. That's why she fights. If she thinks you want her here, she'll come round. Promise.'

'I hope so,' Mom says. 'Because if she *does*, well, this may be a solution.'

'Shall we try it for a month? See how it goes?' Dad asks.

'Mom! Dad!' The stuff I say next is too embarrassing to remember.

46

Sunday morning is such a big deal we actually miss church. Aunt Teddi, Mom and her closest friends have a cleaning bee in the kitchen, dining room, bathroom and powder room, while a few of Dad's buddies bring their trailers to clear out the guest room, attic, basement, back porch, and other spots Granny won't see.

Meanwhile she and I stay at our place going over her albums. I take out her favourite pictures to scan for a tablet slideshow. Every so often, Granny says, 'It's such a shame you didn't grow up at the Bird House.'

'What would you say if I moved in now?'

'I'd say your parents wouldn't be happy.'

'What if they came too? Imagine Dad back home like in the old days?'

Granny smiles. 'I can still see him on the swing that hung from the maple tree; tossing a baseball with your grampa.'

'So it's a yes?'

'Is what a yes?'

'Dad living with us at the Bird House?'

'Your mother wouldn't let him,' Granny says. 'Between

you, me and the fencepost, she doesn't like me. Wants me in a nursing home. Hah!'

'What if I changed her mind? Could she stay with us if I lived with you?'

Granny claps her knees. 'If you lived with me, she could do whatever she pleased.'

We repeat this conversation till Granny falls asleep on the couch. That's when I pack my suitcase. When Aunt Teddi takes us for dinner, my parents pack theirs.

Back at the Bird House, I help Granny get ready for bed while my parents unpack. Aunt Teddi and I tuck her in.

'It's Teddi, Mom.' Teddi kisses her forehead. 'I'll be home again next weekend.'

'Teddi.' Granny smiles. 'Who's that I hear in the guest room?'

'Mom and Dad. We're having a sleepover.'

'How nice. I was afraid it might be your grampa. He needs to stay on the comfy couch.'

My parents say everything's fine; that we should expect a few hiccups. Still, a few of the hiccups are more like heaves. Till the Bird House gets Internet at the end of week one, Dad's without his monitor, which makes for serious *Whew boys*. And when Granny catches Mom meddling in the den, she calls her 'Missy Ferguson'.

'Mom's just trying to help,' I say.

'Is she now?' Granny huffs.

'Granny, say sorry,' I whisper. 'Please? For me?'

'Sorry,' Granny says, like she *so* doesn't mean it.

After, I tell Mom to remember the bargain: she gets to do what she wants in the kitchen, but the den and front yard are out of bounds.

I Skype Aunt Teddi in a panic. 'They're going to pull the plug.'

'Relax,' she says. 'Your parents want this to work.'

'Do they?' My voice is way high.

'Yes. For as long as it can.'

'Which means tomorrow.'

'Your dad said a month. He keeps his word.'

'Hi, Zoe,' Uncle Wilf waves in the background. I try to smile, waving back.

'Wilf and I are coming up this weekend,' Aunt Teddi says. 'Your folks'll have a break. Breaks make a difference.'

They do. Other things do, too. Once we get Internet, Dad has a revelation. Not only is it nicer to work at a window than facing a basement wall, but, 'It's easier to concentrate without that GD hair dryer.' And Mom remembers my biggest Granny tip. 'Don't argue. Just smile and distract.'

Granny chills out. She mostly sits on the rocker or naps on the comfy couch. The odd time she wanders into Dad's office, it's like she's forgotten he ever left home. The one thing that drives us nuts is her repeating herself. When it's too much we give her the tablet with the slideshow.

Her face changes with the photos, as she sits happily, finding herself in the past.

I know we're good the night Mom and Dad ask if it'd be okay if they took a night's break after Granny's in bed.

'D'uh,' I laugh. 'I'm two minutes away.'

Naturally, Mom calls a million times, the first hour. 'Is everything all right?'

'No,' I tease, 'the house is on fire.'

'Do you need anything?'

'Yes, a ladder to get Granny off the chimney.'

'Not funny. If you need anything—'

'What I really need is peace and quiet.'

'Is Granny disturbing you?'

'No. It's just the phone keeps ringing.'

'Oh. Okay. Sorry. Love you, honey.'

It's sweet how they think I need them. Which, okay, maybe I do. But with the three of us, plus Aunt Teddi and Uncle Wilf, we have things under control.

Wednesday, a few months after the move, Granny and I are on the front lawn adjusting Fred's tie. Granny looks up at the sky. 'They say every star is an angel waiting to be born.'

'Who's they?'

'You know,' Granny says like I'm an idiot. 'The folks that write the baby cards.'

'Imagine if it was true: all those angels looking down at the Bird House.'

'Why, where else would they look? The Bird House is the finest house ever. It's where I live. It's where I'm going to die, too.'

'That's right, Granny. But not for a long time.'

'A long *long* time.'

CODA

Life is a storybook. Our stories depend on what happens and what doesn't; what we know and what we don't; what we forget and why. That's what makes telling the truth tricky. Because the past never stays still: it keeps changing into the future.

I like to end the story of Granny and me with us in the front yard looking up at the stars. That's a happy ending, a real one, and a true one. But it's not the only one. Other times my mind keeps going, and the story isn't as easy. On times like those, I remember an ending more like this:

Granny was stable for another six months. She dressed herself except for my help with the armholes, socks and laces, and she mostly made it to the toilet on time. Thank God for track pants.

There were difficult times, sure, but then she'd say, 'You're so good to me,' and I'd say, 'You're so good to be good to,' and I felt so tender, I wouldn't have traded the hard parts for the world.

Mom and Dad were amazing. Aunt Teddi too. She

Skyped most days and came up with Uncle Wilf every other weekend to give us a break.

'Have you ever thought about working with seniors when you grow up?' Aunt Teddi asked. 'You have a gift.' That made me want to learn from Granny even more, and to study harder at school; which, by the way, was suddenly way more fun.

For one thing, Madi never came back. After she finished community service – picking up trash on Main Street – she went to a boarding academy. According to Aunt Jess, our high school wasn't good enough, ha ha. Also, Ricky and I became friends. That's all, but it was fine. I didn't have time for a boyfriend then.

Granny started to talk more about her parents and grandparents. Not in the past, but in the present and future. 'If you don't see me tomorrow, it's because Grandpa Avis has taken me to the farm.' She said that a lot. Also, 'Mother's coming for dinner. I have to pick rhubarb.'

She also got confused about Mom, who did her hair and nails. Sometimes she'd call her Mona. Aunt Teddi said that Granny had gone to a Mona's Hair and Beauty Salon in Elmira. I remember being afraid there might be a time when she'd mix *me* up.

One day I came home from school and she was so angry. 'Why don't you ever visit?'

It was like I'd been kicked in the stomach. 'I do, Granny. I'm here every day.'

'So you say.'

I brought in a bird's nest from the verandah. She got so excited she forgot she'd been mad. 'You're so good to me,' she said.

'You're so good to be good to.'

Everything was more or less fine until she banged her knee on the piano. The doctor said nothing was pulled or broken but she developed a limp. It didn't affect her moving around; like before, she went from one piece of furniture to the next, using them as supports. But the stairs were a problem.

She seemed to know it, too. Without being told, she started to go up and down on her bum, one step at a time. But because her skin was so thin, it rubbed her tailbone raw. We put on salve and bandages, but we worried about infection. Dad asked if we should put up a children's barrier. 'No,' I said. 'She'd try to climb over and hurt herself for sure.'

For the first time, I wondered if Greenview really *would* be best. We had a family meeting. We agreed that Granny would never be happy except for here, so she should stay: if worse came to worst, she'd have died as she wanted. Only then we asked if we'd forgive ourselves. And *then* we asked why we should think about ourselves at all.

Sometimes there's no good answer. Those are the hardest times of all.

I tried an experiment. Granny already napped on the comfy couch, so I made it up like a bed and put her photos on the coffee table. Somehow a switch turned on. Like Grampa, she stopped using the stairs. The den became her bedroom.

Without the stairs, Granny didn't get much exercise. The less she moved, the less she could. Aunt Teddi rented a hospital bed with adjustable positions; and arranged for a helper to come morning and night.

There was another family meeting, this time with the doctor. The whole time I had to think about life without Granny. Because that's where this was headed. When Granny watched the slideshow, her expression didn't change. She still smiled at me, but she didn't really talk much any more.

We decided to place a Do Not Resuscitate order if Granny's heart stopped. I felt sick to my stomach, but the doctor explained that resuscitation hardly ever works with seniors. Ribs are cracked. Organs are pierced. People die horrible deaths. We didn't want that for Granny.

I kept studying at Granny's bedside. When I needed a break, I'd rub moisturiser into her skin so it wouldn't tear, and rolled her onto different sides so she wouldn't get bed sores. All of us did. I don't think she noticed.

I must have been exhausted, but that's not how I remember it. What I remember is feeling so lucky I had someone like Granny to care for.

The hardest part was getting her to eat. She was thin as sticks. Earlier we'd had a game where she'd take a bite when I would. Then, when she wouldn't lift her fork or spoon, I'd feed her with a different game: the spoon was me coming to the Bird House and her mouth was the front door opening to let me in.

Now though, the front door only opened for a few spoons of apple sauce and soup a day. She'd turn her head away. I was so upset. I remember the day I said: 'Granny, if you don't eat, you'll die.'

Granny smiled like she knew what I was saying, and maybe she did, but she didn't answer. She'd stopped speaking. The next time I put the spoon to her lips, she clenched her teeth and turned her head away.

The doctor said there was nothing anyone could do to force her to eat, unless we wanted to put her in the hospital and stick her full of tubes. Nobody wanted to be that cruel, especially when he said, 'Even then, it won't be long.'

The school gave me permission to be away. I collected my reading and homework assignments for the next week, but the teachers said not to worry, they understood.

I sat by Granny's bed, trying to study, but it was hard not knowing how much longer before I'd never be doing it again.

Aunt Teddi and Uncle Wilf came up. They and my parents sat with Granny in rotation: I stayed non-stop on a recliner. Dad told me I should go upstairs to sleep.

'I can't. I have to be here.'

'It's okay, honey,' Mom said. 'Your granny doesn't know we're here.'

'You don't know that.'

Granny's lips got very dry. We kept them moist with foam Q-tips dipped in sugared water and cooled her forehead with a damp facecloth. Mostly, though, we held her hand and told her the stories she'd told us about her growing up and stories about the wonderful things she'd done for us and how we loved her.

Sometimes it was hard to tell if Granny was still breathing. She'd stop for what seemed like for ever and then she'd start again. The sound was awful.

It happened Saturday morning. Granny and I were alone. My hand was under hers; her eyes were closed.

'Granny,' I said, 'I don't know if you can hear me, but if you can, I want you to know that there will never be anyone like you again, and that I will always, always love you no matter what, just like you loved me.'

There was a pause, and then out of nowhere, Granny opened her eyes. She stared right into mine. She saw me. She knew me. I know it. She squeezed my hand hard.

'Granny. I'm here.'

Her mouth opened. *Pie*.

A curtain fell behind her eyes and she was gone.

I didn't cry. Not then. I just kissed her forehead and sat with her, holding her hand, stroking it with my thumb. It felt like she was still in the room. 'Granny, I'm here,' I said. 'Don't worry. I'll make sure everything's perfect.'

Then I called the others. Their eyes welled up, but

nothing more. It was such a release. Dad phoned the funeral home. The next day, Granny was ready for cremation. I made sure she was dressed in her plaid skirt and the red purse she slung over her shoulder; Aunt Teddi kept her scarf, like she'd have wanted. I put a picture of us all in her hands.

Granny looked like she did when she was asleep on the comfy couch. I stroked her hair. She wasn't there now. All the same I whispered, 'It's okay, Granny. I'll take care of you to the end.'

I told Mom and Dad I wanted to be at the cremation. They didn't know if they could handle it. I said I'd understand if they stayed home, but I had to be there to know everything went right. They decided to come with me. So did Aunt Teddi. They were glad they did.

The operator was very nice. He slid Granny's coffin into the chamber just so and closed the door. We said a prayer. It was time. I asked if it would be okay for me to start things. The operator said yes. As I pressed the button, Granny filled me up: *Thank you.* The world was sky.

Back at the Bird House, we scattered Granny's ashes around the birdbaths and feeders and the bottom of the drain spout where Granny and I searched for elves. I couldn't have imagined it better.

I think a lot about Granny's story – her stories. I wonder about the stories I'll never know from before I was born.

I think about my stories, too: the ones Granny will never know; that even I don't know yet.

Mostly I think about the stories we shared: the ones that run through my mind like that piece of music you never forget.

I miss Granny. I always will. But not in a sad way. More in wonder, I guess, that Granny and I are together whenever I think of her, even when I'm alone.

Thanks

Many thanks to Karen Mcgavin and Tim Rivers of Covenant House, James O'Donnell of Artatorture Tattoo Studio, Jo Altilia of Literature for Life, Connie Vanderfleen of Community Care Access Centre, Dr Sam Munn, the Canada Council for the Arts, the Ontario Arts Council, the Toronto Arts Council, Chloe Sackur, Michelle Anderson, Julie Neubauer, and as always, Daniel Legault and Mom.

A chat with
Allan Stratton

Where did the original idea for *The Way Back Home* come from?

I'd written a few pages of a teen diary for an adult novel. I loved the character to bits – she was so vulnerable and edgy – and I wanted to know her more.

How did the book develop?

With tonnes of conversations with my editor, Charlie. Great editors are like great teachers: they tell you what you need to hear whether you like it or not.

Granny and Teddi weren't characters in the first draft! Zoe ran away on her own and her story followed her random encounters. She was angry, but only for herself. Halfway through, both my editor and I realised the book was missing a core relationship to care about. In the course of brainstorming, I thought of my mom who died of Alzheimer's and who'd hated the idea of being in a nursing home. Suddenly Granny was born, and things fell into place.

If Zoe's relationship to Granny is based on your relationship with your mom, how much of the novel is true?

Like Zoe says at the end, truth is slippery. I'd say it's true emotionally and in some of the details and dialogue, but not in the overall plot.

Like Zoe, I was the only person Mom trusted. When she'd get angry, I'd ask myself why *I'd* be upset if I were her. How would I feel if people I thought were strangers woke me up and tried to undress me for a bath? Why would I want company in the toilet? Why wouldn't I want a doctor to ask me questions? Imagining from her point of view, she made total sense.

One of the true scenes: I went to the cremation, made sure her coffin was straightened, and pressed the button. I'd fought for Mom for years as she'd fought for me when I was little. It was something I wanted and needed to do. I'm so glad I did. After, like Zoe says, the world was sky.

***The Way Back Home* doesn't shy away from big themes like family dysfunction, bullying, and discrimination. Do you start with themes? Are there particular ideas you want to impart?**

No, I only think about character and story: themes emerge from that, not the other way around. I compare it to running a race: you focus on the finish line; sweat flows as a natural byproduct. For me, story is the race; themes emerge on their own from that.

That said, I call my books my 'brain babies' because they come out of my head – and what comes out of anyone's head is connected to their experience. So the stories and characters I write about are always rooted in my life. In that way, I suppose, the themes in my novels are the themes in my life. Whatever's imparted is unconscious; it's in how my readers interpret the way I see life.

You started as an actor and playwright. Does that influence the way you write novels?

Absolutely. Writing first person is like writing a monologue. And for every character in every scene I ask, 'What do I want? What am I going to do to get what I want?' Imagining myself into the characters makes writing like a one-person improv. On my best days, it's like I'm not even writing; the characters are speaking and I find myself laughing, frightened and crying by the things they say – sometimes secrets I hadn't even imagined. Those days are magic.

Any advice for your writers?

First. Read, read, read. Write, write, write.

Second. When in doubt, cut it out. Gardens look so much better when they've been weeded.

Third. Read your work aloud. Privately, it helps enormously in catching errors and in getting your rhythms right. With friends, it lets you know what parts are working and what parts are putting people to sleep!